…drifting up and down his arm was making it impossible for Adam to concentrate on the movie. That and his preoccupation with watching Marc drink from his pop. Here he was, a notorious womanizer; and he was getting a hard-on because some guy was sipping on his straw.

Adam took the drink back, slipping the straw between his lips. He could taste Marc on it. And he tasted incredible. The image of Marc sucking on his dick, the same way he'd been sucking on that straw, flashed through his mind, and he just about creamed his pants. Marc's warm breath whispered across Adam's ear followed by his voice. "You're making those incredible noises again."

"Christ, Marc. I don't know what's gotten into me." Adam closed his eyes, waiting for the obvious retort to that statement, but it never came. Marc would never be that crass. He was a gentleman. A true gentleman that was interested in him. Wanted him. And it felt really good.

POSSESSION

POINTE

Leigh Jarrett

www.leighjarrett.com

Published by Steambath Press

Contact: steambathpress@hotmail.com

Possession Pointe; Combined Edition

Leigh Jarrett

Copyright © 2012 by Leigh Jarrett

Paperback:

ISBN-13: 978-1927553107

ISBN-10: 1927553105

First published (eBook) August 2012

ISBN: 978-1-927553-08-4

Chapter One

The hardwood floors creaked happily beneath Adam O'Neill's feet, making him feel at home. It was early. The sun had only just risen above the horizon as the mandatory pot of coffee began spitting and steaming. Its aroma drifted out from the back office, mingling with the lingering scent of resin and sweaty young bodies. Adam set his posture and studied himself in the panel of full length mirrors that ran from one end of the ballet studio to the other.

They were all the same. Not the mirrors. Ballet studios. Worn wooden floors, stretching out from beneath massive warehouse windows. High barre on one side of the room. Mirrors on the other. Dusty little rosin box in the corner. Check. Decrepit piano. Check. Predictable. Yes. But also comforting. Especially when you were starting off in a new city with a new ballet company.

Adam rose up on the balls of his feet and tested the give in the floor. It sprung back nicely, tempting him to begin his warm-up before he'd downed his first; make that third cup of coffee. He might even forego his next cigarette if he became distracted enough.

"What do you think?"

"The lighting is good," Adam said, turning to face Carolyn; his new ballet mistress and, as his finances required, new boss. He'd moved clear across the country after a closed audition had landed him the principal male role in one the fledging company's productions. A lofty accomplishment, except he needed to eat and have a roof over his head; something not attainable strictly on a dancer's wage. He had arranged to teach a few classes for Carolyn to supplement his income. The first of which was due to start in twenty minutes.

"Are you prepared for this first lot of students?" Carolyn asked; her eyes crinkling merrily at the corners. She could barely contain herself. "They'll definitely present you with that 'challenge' you were so anxious to undertake."

"Not quite what I had in mind when I said it." Adam set his posture in front of the mirrors again, examining his lines. He rolled his eyes as the first of his alleged 'students' came barrelling loudly through the doors, shoving and jostling their immense bodies against each other and dropping their bags like weighted sacks of potatoes.

"Gentlemen!" Adam shouted as he clapped his hands together briskly. "This is a ballet studio. Not a football stadium. Kindly keep your voices down." He spun back towards the mirror, annoyed, and caught a glint of amusement in Carolyn's eye. "What?"

"Nothing." Carolyn smiled knowingly. "I think, perhaps, these young men will be begging their coach for a reprieve from 'ballet hell' once you're through with them."

Adam frowned, dipping his eyebrows. "You know what they're probably thinking, don't you? That they're big football stars, and what we do here, in this studio, is for sissies." He set his shoulders, prepared. "They'll be lucky to walk out of here alive."

"Of that I have no doubt." Carolyn patted Adam's shoulder, reassured that he'd definitely been the right choice. "I'm heading out for a smoke. Are you coming?"

"And let the hellions run free. I think not." Adam grinned at Carolyn, loosening up slightly. "I'm trying to cut back."

"What kind of dancer are you?" Carolyn asked as an unlit cigarette bobbled about in her mouth, immediately endearing her to Adam. His very first ballet mistress had wandered about the studio with an unlit cigarette dangling from her lips. That had been twenty five years ago, and he hadn't looked back. Ballet was his entire life now and he couldn't imagine doing anything else. It was his true love.

"Next you'll be telling me you're thinking about giving up coffee," Carolyn continued as she headed for the door.

"Ha!" Adam coughed out. "My life blood... never." He rotated his neck to relieve the stress as he watched Carolyn leave. Three more men had arrived. They were quieter than the first two, but there were supposed to be eight of them in all. He checked the clock. Tardiness was high on his irritation list. Luckily, one more stepped through the door before Adam strode over and locked it. Carolyn would have to come back in through the office after she finished her smoke. He had certain expectations. If his students couldn't be bothered coming on time, then why should he be bothered teaching them? Respect and discipline. Cornerstones of his world that these football hooligans would have to get through their thick heads.

Adam clapped his hands loudly, startling the six men standing idly by the windows, peering down at the street below. *Perhaps warming up might've been a better idea.* Even his five year old students knew that. He brushed off the thought. His own son would be turning five soon. Joyous, except he wouldn't be there to celebrate his only child's birthday. Too far away and too little money.

"Gentlemen," Adam began, speaking briskly. "Bare feet please, no talking and take your places at the barre."

A snort of laughter had Adam grinding his teeth in annoyance. *No, not that kind of bar.* He batted his eyelashes, dimpled his cheeks and withdrew his cane from behind his back, cracking it sharply across the front of the piano with stunning results. Their coach probably didn't carry one of those around. The threat of getting their little asses whipped had definitely got their attention.

"Places please," Adam repeated and smiled demurely as the panic stricken men figured out what a barre was and attempted to stand correctly at it. He approached them with the optimum speed and direction to make them feel uneasy. It was a skill really. The first man jumped as he stepped up behind him. "Name please."

"Ted... sir," the first man said, uncertain of the protocol.

"Lovely, Theodore. Thank you." Adam stepped up behind the next man and adjusted the spacing between the two. When the man didn't speak, Adam tapped him lightly on the ass with his cane.

"Sorry. The name's Bill... sir."

Adam nodded and stepped forward to the next man in line, but looked back over his shoulder. "Stand up straight please, William. You don't have permission to slouch just because I'm not looking."

"Yes, sir—"

"Master O'Neill." Adam said as he perused the man standing barely a step in front of Bill. "While in class, you will all refer to me as Master O'Neill." He directed the current man to take a few steps forward. Why on earth people felt the need to bunch up like that he'd never understand. Better to be independent and have the freedom to move around. Free as a bird. After two failed marriages, that was his new motto. "What's your name, sweetheart?"

"Marc, sir... short for Marco, not Marcus."

"Well, Marc, short for Marco, not Marcus, you need to stay well away from William here, unless, of course, you were hoping he'd fuck you the next time you bent over."

Adam let the rush of coughs and groans of amusement go unchecked. He wasn't a complete monster. Classes with him could be fun as long as everyone remembered who was in charge. He hadn't meant to pick on the man lighting up his gaydar, but in his world, gay men made up a large percentage of its male population and they were used to the ribbing. Expected it actually, and dished it out as readily as received it. It was part of their everyday banter. The comment had slipped out as naturally as breathing.

"That's enough boys," Adam said as he tapped the floor with his cane, striding forward to the next student. "Name please."

Once the names were gathered and everyone was evenly spaced, Adam stood back to examine his group. It was obvious that these weren't players from their defensive line. They were too leanly muscled to offer any kind of forceful resistance. These were their runners and receivers. These boys needed to learn how to fly; gracefully, and land without breaking anything. Two things he was very good at.

"Turn your heads, not your bodies. Watch me please. We're going to start in first position of the feet. Like so." Adam placed his feet and waited for the men to copy. "One hand on the barre. The other in first position of the arms."

Lord help me. They've all got two left everything.

"Quickly please, gentlemen. If this is all we get done today, I'll have to take a Valium to soothe my nerves."

Walking down the line, Adam checked the positioning and posture of each man. Making slight adjustments as a means to exert his authority rather than correct; although they were responding well.

"Your hand should be resting lightly on the barre. I don't want to see anyone gripping it like their dick on a lonely Saturday night."

This statement brought on a round of snorting that had Adam smiling. He might actually have fun teaching these guys. They were boorish, but then, who was he kidding, so was he. One of the many reasons both his wives had left him. That and the smoking, drinking and general fucking around behind their backs. But those days were behind him. As long as he remained single, he felt no inclination to smoke, drink and fuck around. Well, maybe smoke, but that was it. For some reason, having a woman tied around his neck made him crazy. Drove him to do stupid things. He was better off alone. At least that's what he kept telling himself.

"We are going to start with plies in first position. Which in lay man's terms means you are going to bend your knees, without sticking your ass out, and you're going to keep your knees nicely placed over your toes." Adam's eyes narrowed. Young Theodore appeared to be balking at the idea of doing plies. "The reason we do this exercise is to strengthen the muscles we require to keep our knees nicely placed over our toes at all times."

Ted exhaled sharply, turning away from the barre. "Why? Why the fuck should I care about that?"

"Firstly, because, I swear to God... if you ever speak to me like that again, I will cane you, and secondly, because doing so will reduce the chance of you fucking up your knees next time you land a pass."

"Coach already explained all this, Ted," Bill said, peering over his shoulder, not wanting to mess up what he'd achieved by turning around. "Flexibility, core strength... agility. It's all good stuff."

Marc grunted and exhaled heavily through his nose.

"Did you have something to add, Marco, not Marcus?" Adam asked as he stepped in to adjust Marc's posture. He tucked the cane under his arm, running one hand up Marc's chest to encourage him to straighten up, and the other hand down his back, pressing Marc's ass back under his hips. "You need to keep your ass tucked under. If you keep tipping your hips back like that, people are going to talk." *And so they should with an ass like that.*

Stepping back, Adam looked at Marc, who was blushing furiously. *Christ. I said that out loud, didn't I?*

Typical. Absolutely fucking typical. Would you like to embarrass yourself on the very first day of work, Adam? Yes, sir. Yes, please, sir.

"Center floor, gentlemen. No talking."

Marc fussed about with his bag, stalling for time as the other men gathered up their stuff and headed out the door. They would wait for him outside. The plan was to go for breakfast, but he needed to talk to their instructor first. He was having trouble believing that someone that beautiful could be such an asshole.

"Did you wish to speak with me, Marc?" Adam asked. His back was turned to the room, but he'd caught Marc watching him in the mirror. He was attempting to begin his own center floor warm-up; unsuccessfully. Marc's roving eyes were distracting him.

Adam let his gaze drift over his own features. There was nothing extraordinary about him. His body was developed as a dancer's should be, and his hair and eyes were an unremarkable brown. He'd often been told he was 'boy pretty'. Whatever that meant, he wasn't sure, but over the years he'd received his share of attention from the gay men he worked with, and he'd soon learned how to handle them. He directed his gaze back at Marc. Better to get it over with now, otherwise the obvious attraction Marc felt for him might flourish unchecked.

"Marc," Adam began. "I'd like to apologize for calling you out in front of the class today; twice, no less. But after the first remark seemed to amuse your team mates to no end, I assumed they already knew." He turned to face Marc and tilted his head. "Again, I apologize. I didn't mean to make you feel uncomfortable."

Adam tucked his arms across his chest. A stance unfamiliar to him, but Marc's steady, hungry gaze was making his gut twinge. He pinched his face up, confused. "Was there something else?"

"We were wondering if you wanted to come to breakfast with us."

"Oh—"

"The guys all thought it would be a good idea. Maybe you wouldn't bust our balls so bad next week."

"That's unlikely to be the case," Adam replied, amused. "I suppose breakfast would be alright though." He hadn't eaten anything that morning yet. Not an unusual practice for him, but agreeing to head out for breakfast with people, who were practically strangers, was extremely unusual. He'd only been in the city for a week, but perhaps it was time to start making some friends. But football players? *Sure, what the hell. Hot football players could be his thing.*

Adam's face flushed. *Fucking hell. I said that out loud too.*

"I'm sorry," Adam said as he tried to regain his composure. "Sometimes my mind and my mouth have a miscommunication problem. Thinking inwardly doesn't always work."

Marc shrugged his shoulders. "No problem. At least that way, I'll always know what you're thinking—" He paused, eyebrows raised expectantly, unsure as to what he should be calling him now that class was over.

"Adam. Outside the studio, my name's Adam."

"Nice to meet you, Adam." Marc clasped his hands together. "So, let's get going. The guys will be waiting for us downstairs."

"Just let me slip on some street clothes."

Predictably, Adam's sweat pants were at the bottom of his bag, forcing him to dig for them. A handful of brightly coloured jockstraps landed on the floor. That probably wasn't going to help his case any, but he couldn't help it if he had a saucy side. Finding the worn gray sweats, he pulled them on over his tight black leggings. *No sense in subjecting Marc to my bulge during breakfast. Although, I certainly enjoyed the attention it was receiving.* Christ. Where the fuck had that come from?

"I wasn't sure you'd noticed," Marc said and then his lips twitched knowingly. "You did it again… the talking thing."

"For the love of Pete." Doing a perfect 'face palm', Adam turned to face the mirror, preferring not to make direct eye contact with Marc. The guy was seriously flustering him. His mouth wasn't usually this unruly, and neither was his mind. "Marc, I think I should explain to you why I joined ballet in the first place."

"Sure." Following Adam's direction, Marc took a seat on the piano bench. "Although I would assume it's because you like dancing."

"No, that came later. See, when I was nine years old, my mother took me to my very first ballet. I was in awe of the principal male *danseur*, and not for the reason you're currently assuming." Adam shifted uncomfortably from one foot to the other; suddenly unsure as to whether or not he wanted to be telling Marc this.

"There he was," Adam continued, "dressed in his elegant costume, strong and confident at the center of the stage, girls spinning delicately around him, fawning over him and desiring his attention." Adam sighed for emphasis. "To a nine year old boy, that had developed a little earlier than his friends, it was pretty powerful stuff. The thought of having all those girls dancing around me, desiring my attention, and being required to lift them up into the air with hands that were permitted to run over their thinly clothed bodies; it was like discovering the keys to a candy store."

"So, you're not into guys. I'm sorry. I just assumed." Marc laughed softly, resigned, but unconvinced. "I started playing football for a similar reason. Twelve years old. My dad took me to a college football game. I was fixated on the quarterback receiving the ball from the center. The thought of running the back of my hand down a guy's ass crease to receive the ball was my inspiration." He leaned back against the piano keys, jumping when they sounded off. "How did your dream work out?"

"For the most part, the girls all thought I was gay. So they didn't come anywhere near me, except to be my 'friend'. I had my very own troupe of 'faghags' following me around before I was ten." Adam grinned as Marc creased up laughing. "As soon as I was old enough, I had to do some serious fucking around to change their minds. What about you? Any willing ass creases in your career choice?"

"God, no," Marc replied emphatically. "The very idea of imagining my team mates in that light turns my stomach."

"So, lesson learned. Do not determine your life's work on the advice of your dick. They should teach that in school."

"Mm… so true, although I love playing professional football." Marc lifted his cell phone from his pocket. "The guys got tired of waiting for us. They're going to meet us there."

Adam slipped his feet, ballet slippers and all, into a pair of large furry boots and lifted his tattered but adequate coat from the floor. "Okay, let's go."

They decided to walk. It wasn't that far to the diner, and it was daylight. That was the other thing about ballet studios. They were always located in the worst possible neighbourhoods. It was nice to have Marc at his side; his very own protector; even though the guy was probably a good ten years younger than him. Adam tilted his gaze to watch Marc's form as they walked down the street. Marc might be an offensive player, but he was built like a house. A sexy, dark haired, blue eyed house, but a house none the less.

"So, truthfully, why were you hovering after class?" Adam asked as he lit up a cigarette. "It wasn't just about breakfast, was it?"

Marc grinned. "I was going to ask you out."

"Really." Adam stopped his progress, picking the bit of tobacco that his filterless cigarette had relinquished, from his tongue. Someday, fortune willing, he'd have enough money to buy proper cigarettes. "Where were you going to take me?"

"I was thinking a movie," Marc replied, jogging to catch up with Adam, who'd started walking again.

"Which movie?"

"I don't know. Maybe 'Warrior Inferno'. I was going to ask you what you wanted to see."

Adam stepped through into the diner as Marc held the door open for him. "I wouldn't mind seeing that actually. My roommate, Kelsey Stickle... I've known her since college. And I just moved to Vancouver from back east, so she's letting me stay with her until I get my own place. Totally platonic of course." *Why the fuck are you telling him that? Like he'd care whether or not you're banging your roommate. Moron.*

"Kelsey; she hates action movies," Adam continued. "She used to drag me to the most nauseating romantic comedies back in the day. They're really not my thing. Way too girly for my liking." *Now you're rambling like an imbecile. Pull it together, asshole.* "Anyways, I don't know anyone in Vancouver yet, except her, and I hate going to see movies alone."

"Did you want to go with me then?" Marc slipped into a booth next to one of his teammates. Dropping into the seat across from Marc, Adam couldn't help but notice the plethora of expectant faces staring at him. *Great. Just what I need. An audience.*

"Yeah, sure," Adam said and then cringed at the response.

"Score," Ted shouted, leaning over the divider of the adjoined booths and slamming his hand down on Marc's shoulder. "I told you not to sweat it, didn't I? Didn't I say he was into you?"

"Would you relax, Ted," Marc replied, lifting Ted's hand away. "Adam and I—" Closing his eyes, Marc shook his head in exasperation as a taunting chorus of 'Oh, Adam and I' surrounded him. "We're just going as friends. Adam's not gay, alright?"

"Well, that's no fun," Ted said, dropping back into his seat.

"Yeah, we were looking forward to harassing you," Bill added as he perused the menu. "I had a whole selection of 'twinkle toes' remarks ready and waiting."

Marc snorted happily. "Thanks a lot guys. It's nice to know you've got my back... or my backside as the case may be."

"Only for you, baby," someone chimed in, but Adam couldn't see who'd spoken. Marc was fortunate to have such a tight group of friends. He'd seen a lot of guys side railed after 'coming out' to their friends, but then maybe Marc had never been 'in' in the first place. He appeared to be one of the lucky ones.

"What are you going to have?" Marc asked Adam, breaking his thoughts. "I'm going for the full deal. Eggs, pancakes, sausage, bacon and hash browns."

"Good Lord," Adam said as he raised his coffee cup into the air, waggling it at the waitress to get her attention. His coffee high was waning. "I'll just have toast."

"I guess you have to keep your body all slim like that?" Marc asked as his gaze drifted over Adam's features; his desire overtly evident. Adam's heart shuddered unexpectedly, sending shivers down his spine as he recognized the depth by which he was being scrutinized. And the reason behind it.

And that he liked it.

Adam just about dropped his freshly filled coffee crashing onto the table, in utter shock, as he felt his balls warm. *Seriously? What the fuck was that about?* Thirty four years as a straight man and now suddenly his body decides to act up?

"I'm not very hungry," Adam answered, finally, after distracting himself. The truth was, the only money he had, in its entirety, was the small amount of change drifting around in the pocket of his sweats. Not enough to buy anything more than coffee and toast, and even then, he wasn't entirely sure he could cover it.

When the food arrived, Adam dove into the carousel of condiments, removing every last offering of peanut butter. He desperately needed the protein. Confused, he looked up as a strip of bacon, a pancake, and a sausage were discreetly slipped onto his plate.

"I can't eat all this," Marc explained, unconvincingly.

What an absolute sweetheart. "Thanks. It's been a while."

Marc grunted softly and dug into his food, leaving Adam to examine his plate; his mouth watering over the virtual feast in front of him. He wondered if anyone would notice if he tucked the pancake away for later, but then decided he wanted to enjoy it now instead. The thought of smothering its hot goodness in butter and syrup had his heart racing. He peered up at Marc, picturing him smothered head to toe in liquid butter and warm maple syrup. Rivulets of lickable sweetness running seductively down Marc's chest, sticking the little hairs together, and curling around what he was certain would be a thick, luscious cock. *Christ. Now that would be a feast and a half.* If he was gay that is. Which he wasn't.

"You need to stop moaning like that," Marc whispered. "The guys are going to hear you. And you're making me hard."

"I'm sorry. I think the stress of moving is getting to me. My mind is playing tricks on me, and I'm seriously falling for them."

"Hm... how's tonight sound for that movie?"

Adam's dick twitched, and he just about burst into tears. The low husky tone of Marc's voice was giving him heart palpitations. *This wasn't happening. This couldn't be happening. Not with a guy.* "Yeah, tonight's good. Maybe we could go for coffee after?"

"Sounds good." Marc was smiling with far too much enthusiasm for Adam's liking. "I'll give you my cell number," Marc continued, undeterred by Adam's 'deer caught in the headlights' expression. "We'll work out the details over the phone after I find out where the movie is playing."

"It's playing at the Paramount," Adam said, regaining his comprehension of what was happening. "It's just down the street from where I'm staying. I could walk." *Because there is no way you are picking me up. That would be too much like a date. And this isn't a date, because I don't date guys.*

Marc winked at Adam. "It's a date then."

"It's a date, Adam," Kelsey stated, between giggling gasps of breath, as she snorted gleefully at Adam's predicament.

"It isn't. We agreed that we were only going as friends."

"That was before he caught you groaning at the sight of him covered in whip cream."

"Syrup," Adam corrected, falling backwards into the cushions of the sofa that was doubling as his bed. "Butter and syrup."

"Details, details." Kelsey dropped down beside Adam and threw her arm around his shoulders. "You want him. Admit it."

"Maybe just a little." Adam covered his face with both hands; confused out of his mind. "I just want to taste him. He's got the most luscious lips." He groaned thinking about them. "God. They make me want to run my tongue between them; ever so gently. Just enough to feel the warmth of his breath rolling across mine."

"What about the butter and syrup on his dick? You can't just leave it there. His underwear will get all sticky."

"That was a hypothetical scenario."

"Doesn't have to be." Kelsey snapped her gum loudly. Adam had always hated when she did that. They'd roomed together briefly in college and Kelsey had almost driven him into the insane asylum with her crass personality, gum snapping and bad taste in music. But she was one of the few people that had ever been strong enough to put up with his bullshit attitude and keep coming back for more, and he loved her for it. There weren't too many people around that understood him the way she did. He could tell her anything.

"What do you think dick tastes like?" Adam asked, adjusting himself so he could see Kelsey.

"How the fuck would I know? I'm a lesbian, remember?"

Adam dropped back into the cushions. "I thought maybe you'd at least tried it before you 'decided' to become a lesbian." He ducked as the inevitable smack landed on the side of his head. He honestly couldn't understand the fascination with a women's snatch, especially when you were a woman yourself. Wasn't one snatch enough in a relationship? They were already a high maintenance body part without adding a second one. He should know. Two marriages over the course of six years. That was seventy two weeks of his life lost to raging PMS induced mayhem.

"Drop your pants," Kelsey said sharply.

Adam shot up in his seat. "What for?"

"Drop your pants. I'll suck you off and tell you what it tastes like." Kelsey motioned for Adam to hurry up as he struggled to undo the knot in his sweatpants. That was the other thing he loved about Kelsey. She was a spontaneous nutcase.

"It'll serve two purposes," Kelsey continued while helping Adam to remove his underwear. "I can tell you what it tastes like and you're less likely to start humping young Marco's leg in the movie theatre."

"I have no intention of humping Marc's leg."

"Mm... hm." Kelsey looked up at Adam as she slipped onto the floor at his feet, taking his semi-hard cock into her hand. "I suppose I should take my gum out, hey? Don't need the added choke risk. Looks like you've got a whopper." She grinned and removed the gum, deliberately sticking it to the curly dark hairs of Adam's pubes. Kelsey also had a notable sadistic streak.

"I just had a shower," Adam said, angling his body as Kelsey's tongue enveloped his shaft, licking him from root to tip, and humming, like she was enjoying an ice cream cone on a hot summer day. Suddenly, he wasn't entirely sure she hadn't done this before. "So, that's going to change things somewhat... taste wise."

He dropped his head back as his breathing changed. He hadn't been given a blow job in almost six months; an eternity on the scale of his promiscuous timeline.

"It doesn't actually taste like much," Kelsey said, jacking him gently in one hand. "Kind of neutral actually, if you discount the soapy taste." Adam reached down, enveloping her hand, and encouraged her to stroke him a bit rougher.

"It feels nice on my tongue though," Kelsey added, grinning.

Adam sucked air in past his lips, gripping at Kelsey's shoulder as she teased the slit and circled her tongue around the thick ridge. And then without warning, Kelsey smacked her lips together and sat back on her heels. Adam's stomach lurched.

"Why did you stop?"

"You're leaking something." Kelsey leaned in and swiped the flat of her tongue across the head of Adam's dick, and then pumped him a few times. "That pre-cum stuff. Tastes kind of sweet actually. Maybe a little musky." She dipped her finger into his slit and held it up to him. "Taste it."

"No—" Adam crunched up his face. "I'm not tasting my own cum."

Kelsey settled her finger in her own mouth. "Suit yourself, but you're missing out. It tastes really good." Seeing that Adam wasn't buying it, she dove back onto his cock, sucking and slurping noisily; driven by the amazing sounds emanating from the man she considered to be her best friend.

Adam smirked at the sound of Kelsey moaning contentedly as she savoured the experience of making his dick hard. She'd definitely done this before. He groaned as she changed her technique, bringing him closer to the edge. "Fuck, Kelsey. That feels good! What kind of cock sucking lesbian are you anyways?"

Kelsey immediately dropped Adam's cock from her mouth with a loud popping sound. "Do you want me to finish this or not? Because another lesbian crack from you is going to have me reaching for my strap-on."

"God, you don't honestly have one of those, do you?" Adam cringed when Kelsey nodded mischievously. "Well, you can dismiss that thought from your pretty little head, because I'm not interested in bending over for anyone… ever."

"Your dick seems to disagree with you. That little soldier got hard, all on his own, at the mention of a big cock going up your ass."

"Good for the little soldier, but I'm in charge, so no butt sex and no more lesbian cracks, I promise."

"We'll just have to see how strong your resolve is once you get all hot and heavy with young Marco." Kelsey winked at Adam as she took his now rock hard cock back into her mouth. It wasn't long until Adam was swearing and bucking, shooting loads of hot cum down Kelsey's throat. She almost gagged a few times, but managed to swallow most of it down.

"What does it taste like?" Adam asked anxiously. Not sure he really wanted to know if the news was bad.

Kelsey shook her head and climbed back up onto the sofa. She caught Adam completely off guard when she pounced on him, attacking his mouth and forced her tongue past his lips, dispensing a significant snowball in his mouth.

She fell back laughing as Adam sputtered and spat, drawing the back of his hand across his mouth to wipe away the mixture of spit and cum dripping from his mouth.

"So, what does your cum taste like, Adam?"

"Fucking disgusting." Adam spat again. "It's so bitter. Fuck. I can't believe you just did that."

"Don't be such a baby." Kelsey reached for her purse, stuck a new piece of gum into her mouth and lifted her cell phone. "Hey, it's almost eight o'clock. You need to get going, but you should probably brush your teeth first. Your spunk infused breath might turn Marco on, and he'll be looking to fuck you right there in the theatre."

Kelsey shrieked wildly in amusement as Adam made a run for the washroom. "And you'll want to get rid of that gum. It'll be difficult to explain how it got there."

Chapter Two

Adam was freezing by the time he reached the theatre. It was a much longer walk than he'd anticipated, but it had given him a chance to think about things. Getting that blowjob from Kelsey had reminded him how much he liked having a woman's mouth around his cock, and it had relieved some of the sexual pressure that had been building since he'd broken up with his last girlfriend; the latest entry in a long list of meaningless, faceless women.

And that's exactly what he'd spent the majority of his time pondering on the walk over. The history of his love life, in its entirety, was on that list. His relationships were always meaningless, pointless and bloody frustrating. Maybe he was ready for a change. Maybe he needed to find someone that had the ability to understand him on a deeper level. Adam shook his head vehemently. *No. Not going to happen. I like women.*

"Hey, Adam," Marc said, as he stepped away from where he was waiting for Adam by the ticket booth. "I was starting to think you'd changed your mind." He touched Adam's shoulder to move him towards the door. "I bought the tickets already."

"Thanks. But you didn't have to do that." Now what was he supposed to do? He couldn't have Marc paying for everything. That would make this too much like a date; with him being the girl no less. *Absolutely not.*

"Not what?" Marc asked.

"Oh, it's nothing." Adam fidgeted with the worn ten dollar bill he'd borrowed from a reluctant Kelsey, in his jean's pocket. It wouldn't even be enough to buy popcorn for the both of them. He'd only planned on using it for his own admission.

"I'm not hungry," Marc said, nudging in beside Adam, who was staring aimlessly and undecidedly up at the menu board; the prices were ridiculous. "Did you want to just buy yourself a drink or something?"

God, he was precious. "Yeah, I think that's all I need for now."

Arranging his body so Marc wouldn't see the state of the paper money he was handing over, Adam bought a large drink; enough to share. Just in case Marc got thirsty.

The theatre wasn't overly full. There were a significant number of teenagers; mostly boys in large obnoxious groups, and a few couples. Marc led the way down the aisle and stepped towards a row, commanding immediate attention from those seated near the end; probably due to his stature. Or maybe it was the confidence he exuded; tenfold. Adam was a little stunned when Marc reached back for his hand, gripping it softly in his own as he manoeuvred them to their seats. Marc obviously wasn't the kind of guy that hid his orientation. And his hand was so warm and comforting.

Christ! Are you seriously holding his hand? What is wrong with you? Adam snapped his hand back as they tucked into two seats positioned very near the center, and looked around, analyzing the people around them; particularly the ones behind. Not that he was planning on snogging with Marc in the theatre, but he wanted to be aware of his surroundings. An entire lifetime of people thinking he was gay had taught him a few things about protecting himself. *Although.* He looked over at Marc's profile.

God, he really is gorgeous. Adam relaxed into his seat, lifting his drink. He had Marc with him. He didn't need to worry about the people around them.

A young face that had been turning around frequently, since they'd sat down, finally spoke up. "Hey, are you Marc Tucker?"

Marc extended his hand, shaking the one offered him. "Yes, I am. Are you a fan of the team?"

"Definitely. I keep telling my dad that you guys are going all the way to the Grey Cup this year, but he isn't convinced."

"I don't know. I think you're right. We might have a shot."

"We can't lose with a tight end like you."

The mouthful of pop, Adam had just drawn into his mouth, surged out his nose, spraying Marc, himself, and at least three of the people in front of them. He would've been mortified if Marc hadn't been laughing so hard.

"I'm so sorry," Adam eventually gasped out, wiping pop from his face. He accepted the tissue Marc handed him and had a good run at his nose. The pop was fucking painful, buzzing around in his sinuses. "God, you can't take me anywhere, honestly."

Marc leaned his face in close to Adam's and slipped an arm around Adam's shoulders, startling and then settling him. "I think you're adorable. And I'd be proud to take you anywhere."

Christ, he's fucking priceless. Adam dropped his face into Marc's shoulder, laughing. Keeping his thoughts to himself was proving to be a pointless exercise around

Marc. "I should just tape my mouth closed. It would be easier than trying to control it any other way." Marc shook his head and pulled Adam closer. And then the house lights dimmed.

The distraction of Marc's fingertips drifting up and down his arm was making it impossible for Adam to concentrate on the movie. That and his preoccupation with watching Marc drink from his pop. Here he was, a notorious womanizer; and he was getting a hard-on, because some guy was sipping on his straw.

Adam took the drink back, slipping the straw between his lips. He could taste Marc on it. And he tasted incredible. The image of Marc sucking on his dick, the same way he'd been sucking on that straw, flashed through his mind, and he just about creamed his pants. Marc's warm breath whispered across Adam's ear followed by his voice. "You're making those incredible noises again."

"Christ, Marc. I don't know what's gotten into me." Adam closed his eyes, waiting for the obvious retort to that statement, but it never came. Marc would never be that crass. He was a gentleman. A true gentleman that was interested in him. Wanted him. And it felt really good.

Adam almost dropped his key twice; his hands were shaking so badly. Kelsey had paid to have one key cut for him, but neither of them had had enough money to pay for a key ring. Dropping that key likely would've resulted in it slipping through the storm grate, in front of the door to the apartment building, which meant he'd be locked out, because Kelsey was staying at her girlfriend's tonight.

The last thing he wanted to do was embarrass himself in front of Marc, whom, Adam was now realizing, was likely always clean shaven, well dressed and completely put together. And judging by the jewellery, cologne and the car they'd driven over in; Marc was also doing well for himself, moneywise.

Anxiety welled up in Adam's chest at the thought of losing Marc before they'd even begun. Marc was going to realize he'd made a mistake as soon as they walked in that door, wondering what had possessed him to ask an aging, dancing pauper out.

Once inside, Adam directed Marc to the stairs, apprehensive about, but at the same time comforted by, the outstretched hand offered him. He slid his hand into Marc's, exhilarated by the strength and acceptance, and led him up the stairs to the apartment.

"So, what does Kelsey do for a living?" Marc asked, stepping into the cramped bachelor suite. The kitchen consisted of an ancient looking fridge, a two burner stove and a small sink along one wall, directly across from a bank of grubby windows that gaining access to would've involved simply skirting around a tattered sofa and a single mattress pushed into one corner of the room.

"She doesn't," Adam answered as he hauled the coffee maker out of a cupboard under the sink.

"Oh—"

"Kelsey has a scary high IQ, so she doesn't tend to play well with others. She can't keep a job to save her life… literally." Adam managed to plug the coffee pot in, but was having difficulty arranging the filter in it. The shaking in his hands had progressed to his chest, and now it felt like his entire body was vibrating. He'd never been so nervous about anything in his life. The thought of Marc touching him was stirring up some seriously mixed reactions.

"So what does she do for money?" Marc asked; perplexed and appalled by the squalor he was standing amidst.

"Apparently, the 'idiots' of the world irritated her enough that the government now considers her to be disabled. She lives off a federal disability pension." *Fuck!* The coffee scoop had slipped out of his hands, spilling grounds everywhere. The possibility of a nervous breakdown was looming large. He wasn't usually this much of a klutz, but he could barely feel his fingers, and now the numbness was creeping up his left arm. *Fuck, maybe I'm having a stroke. Or maybe it's a heart attack. That's just perfect.*

Adam shrieked in surprise when Marc stepped up behind him and wrapped him up in his arms, resting his chin on Adam's shoulder.

"Relax," Marc said. "This is only our first date."

And that means what exactly?

"It means I'm not going to push you," Marc answered Adam's spoken thought. "And I'm thinking coffee probably isn't the best idea for you right now. I don't want to be peeling you off the ceiling. Do you have anything more soothing to drink?"

Adam nodded his head, leaning back into Marc's chest. The warmth and security of his arms felt amazing. "Kelsey has some scotch hidden behind the fridge."

"Perfect." Marc kissed the back of Adam's head. "Tell her, I'll replace it the next time I come over to see you."

Adam cupped his hand to his mouth. *The next time... you come... see me?* He steadied his breathing. Marc wanted to see him again. His heart skipped a few beats as he leaned against the counter while Marc retrieved the scotch. Watching Marc move the fridge, was like watching someone move an empty box; absolutely effortless. And hot; definitely hot.

"Glasses?" Marc held the bottle up, looking for direction. Adam snapped out of his stupor and lifted two down. Taking his, he followed Marc over to the sofa, tossing his pillow and sleeping bag onto Kelsey's bed before they both sat down.

"Is this where you sleep?" Marc asked as his gaze scrutinized the state of the sofa. "It can't possibly be long enough for you."

"Better than a cardboard box." *Christ, that had just slipped out.*

Marc leaned away from Adam so he could see him better. "You've never... have you?"

There had been a few times in the past when Adam had ended up on the street, but that hadn't happened in years, and it had never been for very long. Adam looked into Marc's eyes. They were soft and concerned, and they were expecting the truth, because the man they belonged to would never offer anything but the truth himself. Adam could see that clearly in Marc's expression.

"There have been a few times when I haven't been able to make rent," Adam answered softly, embarrassed, but strangely relieved to be sharing this part of his life with Marc. A thought occurred to him that he didn't want to be judged for. It never would've happened. "Only when I was single though. When I was married, I always made sure there was enough money. Even if it meant working at McDonalds."

"You were married?"

"Twice… to women, of course." Adam dropped his gaze. *What do you mean 'of course'? There's no 'of course'. It's perfectly legal for gays to get married in this country.*

"Hey, don't sweat it. I just moved here from the states two years ago. I'm still getting used to the concept of equality."

Adam's eyebrows shot up in surprise. *Marc's back had just gone up.* "I'm sorry. I didn't mean to…"

"No, it's alright. Complete equality is one of the many reasons I jumped at the opportunity to move to Canada, but I don't want to talk about it right now." Marc shifted in his seat and crossed his arms in irritation. "Actually—no, I do want to tell you about it."

Marc leaned forward and set his glass down on the floor. "I was raised by two women until I was ten years old; one of them being my birth mother; the other being her life partner, and my other mom. I loved them both… equally. They were my family. I was their son… not just my birth mother's, but theirs… together." He stopped speaking, scrubbing his hand across his face. "When I was ten, my birth mother got sick. Late stage breast cancer. She was dead within three weeks of the diagnosis."

Adam set his drink down, moving closer to Marc, wanting to offer him some level of comfort, but all he could think to do was hold Marc's hand. What else could he do?

"I'm so sorry, Marc," Adam said, meaning it from his very soul. His gut twisted and he shivered; horrified. He had a sinking feeling he knew where this story was going.

"The state took me away… from everything I'd ever known. My home. My friends. What was left of my family. Everything. My other mom had no rights when it came to me. I spent the next six years being jostled around in foster care, because some right wing, righteous bastards thought I'd be better off in the system than with a woman whose only crime was falling in love with another woman."

"God, Marc. I don't know what to say."

Marc fell back into the sofa cushions. "I'm sorry. I didn't mean to unload on you. But that's why, when the opportunity to play for a Canadian team came up, I jumped at it. I had to get the hell out of there. I don't necessarily want to get married or have kids, but I'd like to have the option. Whom I choose to love and spend my life with shouldn't preclude me from having the same rights as every other human being in the country I'm living in."

"I can't imagine what that feels like." Adam tucked in closer to Marc, leaning his head against Marc's shoulder and draped an arm across Marc's chest. He lifted his feet off the floor, pressing into Marc further as he curled up. "I think we get complacent living up here sometimes. We forget not everywhere is like this."

Marc grunted his acknowledgment, relaxing slightly. "Well, I'm here now… and I'm with you. So everything's good."

"Mm.…" *Yeah… it is, isn't it?* Adam rolled in tighter to Marc and wrapped his hand around Marc's strong bicep, pressing his face into Marc's shoulder to inhale the scent of him. *This was alright. He could do this. He really wanted this.*

"Do you have any kids?" Marc asked.

Adam pushed up away from Marc, struggling to pull his wallet out of his jeans. "I have a son; Connor—" He slipped a tenderly worn picture out and handed it to Marc. "He's going to be five soon, and Cathy, my ex, says he's already reading a few words out of his favorite books." He settled back in against Marc's side. "Maybe he'll grow up to be smarter than his old man, and pick a profession that actually pays you money."

"He looks just like you."

"Poor little bugger."

Marc shifted, handing back the picture. "Don't say that. I think you're beautiful."

That was different. Never been called beautiful before. Adam cupped his hands over his face. *Good God... am I blushing?*

Marc's body shook as a wave of gentle laughter rolled through him. "You've really never been with another guy before, have you?"

"Why on earth would I make something like that up?"

"I don't know. Some guys are into that. The thought of popping some guy's cherry makes them hot."

"Are you one of those guys?"

"It's been known to happen, but in your case, *no*, that wasn't my intention when I asked you out."

"Why not?"

Marc barked out a laugh. "Because—" He hugged Adam closer to him. "I'm more interested in you than I am in your cherry. Which leads me to my next decision. I need to get going. I think both of us have pretty early starts in the morning."

"You're not just saying that because I scared you off, are you?"

"Why would you think that?"

"I don't know," Adam said, looking around at the peeling wallpaper, and then at his feet. He was wearing three pairs of socks out of necessity; each sock covering the gaping holes of the other two.

Adam looked up as Marc's fingers grasped his chin, demanding his attention. "This isn't you," Marc said, motioning to the room and tugging on the front of Adam's shirt. He touched Adam's chest. "You, as a person... you're in here. All of this around you is the sacrifice you've made in order to do what you truly love. That's not failure... that's strength... that's passion. And that's what drew me to you. You're a powerful man, Adam. Powerful and passionate. And that's the kind of person I'd like to know better."

"Well, how could I say 'no' to that?" Adam blushed and shielded his eyes. "I was thinking it, so I figured I might as well say it out loud."

Marc bit his bottom lip and grinned. "Do you know what I'm thinking?"

Adam straightened up. Maybe Marc had changed his mind about leaving and was going to ravish him instead. "No."

"I'm thinking I'd like to kiss you before I go." Marc traced a finger across Adam's lower lip. "Would that be alright?"

He's asking my permission? Adam's breath caught as he remembered to draw air into his lungs. Marc was more than he ever could've dreamed possible. He pressed up closer to him, letting Marc's breath warm his lips, and then dove into the promise of something different. Something better. And it was. Gloriously so. The sensation of Marc's mouth on his, moving with his, consuming him, felt like he was coming home at last, but it also felt wrong. So very, very wrong. He shouldn't be doing this. He shouldn't be enjoying this. This was wrong.

Adam pulled away sharply.

"What's the matter?" Marc asked, touching Adam's arm. He drew his hand back when Adam flinched.

"I can't do this." Adam stood up, brushing his hands, anxiously, up and down the side seams of his jeans. "I really like you, Marc. Really, I do… but I can't. I can't do this."

Marc rose to his feet. "Was it something I did?"

"No… god, no." Adam sighed, confusion ravaging his mind. "You're perfect. You're probably everything I've ever wanted, but I can't go there. I want to. I really want to, with you, but—"

"You're scared."

Adam nodded his head. "I'm sorry. I'm so… so sorry."

"I'm not." Marc touched Adam's face, stroking it lightly with his thumb. "I had the privilege of spending time with an amazing person today. I won't ever feel sorry about that."

The sound of the door closing behind Marc released a flood gate, and Adam crashed onto the sofa in tears. *Oh, my god… what is wrong with you? Go after him.* Adam tucked his face further into the cushions.

I can't. I just can't.

Chapter Three

The music echoed throughout the massive open space, creating an environment protected from the outside. Inside that space; the music, the room, the dance; time had no meaning. Life outside the dance ceased to matter. There was only the dancer and the flow of the music; the dancer's body existing purely for the purpose of grace and beauty in the storytelling. A story that had been told a thousand times before. A story of love won and lost; joy, sadness and intense grief. All revealed through the movement of one's limbs, frame and face. The inner soul laid bare for the world to see.

It wasn't perfect yet; the dance. But it was getting better. As the music wound down, Adam stepped away from his ending pose and went looking for his sweat pants. He needed to keep his legs either moving or warm; otherwise they'd start cramping on him, and he really needed a smoke break, which meant going outside into the cold. He squinted at the clock. It was ten past seven in the morning. He'd only been in the studio for two hours. He had a lot more to go over before his first class arrived.

Adam had been trying to keep himself occupied since his disastrous date with Marc; the feel of Marc's firm body and soft words haunting him whenever he wasn't distracted. Aside from the two times when his wives had thrown him out of the house, that had to have been one of the worst nights of his life. Poor Kelsey had come home, unexpectedly, to find him in a full blown meltdown. He'd never felt so confused. He desperately wanted to be with Marc, but his upbringing and his entire belief system wouldn't allow it. It just wasn't to be.

Fuck, I need a smoke. Throwing on his boots, Adam headed for the door, barrelling out onto the fire escape; straight into Marc, who'd been hovering outside; startling him.

"Sorry," Adam said. "I didn't mean to run you over." He leaned against the railing and lit his cigarette. "What are you doing here?"

"The front door was locked, but I figured you were here." Marc lifted a brown paper bag. "The guys and I were at a bakery down the street buying breakfast, and I thought I'd pick you up a little something… as friends." He opened the bag and tipped it forward so Adam could see inside. "It's just a couple of bagels; one with cream cheese and lox, and the other with just cream cheese. I wasn't sure if you liked salmon, but figured I'd risk it."

"No, I love salmon." Adam accepted the bag, clutching it to his chest. *How had he managed to say 'no' to this incredibly gentle and caring man?* "Thank you. I really appreciate it." He took a long draw off his cigarette, finishing it, and then flicked it onto the pavement below. "Carolyn tells me you've been out of town for a few days. You had some… away games?"

"Yeah, we had two games in Alberta. Won one, lost one."

"I guess that's the way it goes." Adam tucked himself protectively against the heavy metal door. The wind was picking up. "Did you want to come inside? You could sit with me while I eat these."

"No, I have to get going. We have practice in an hour."

"Then I guess I'll see you in class on Thursday."

"Actually, coach is going to phone Carolyn today to see if we can switch to Friday mornings."

"Oh—" Adam clenched his teeth in an attempt to keep his jaw from trembling, but there was no containing his lips. They pinched and twisted, pursing against each other; giving away Adam's thinly veiled disappointment.

"I have rehearsal on the other side of town every Friday morning. I wouldn't be teaching your class anymore."

"That's not going to mess up your wages, is it?" Marc stepped forward, touching Adam's arm. "Maybe I can talk to the coach. Ask him to re-arrange the training schedule."

Adam shook his head. "No, it's fine. I'll still get paid. Carolyn will let me take over a different class. Don't worry about me."

"I can't help it." Marc traced his hand down Adam's arm and grasped at Adam's fingers. "I can't stop thinking about you."

Sagging against the railing, Adam clung to it, desperate for its support. His heart felt as if it were being torn in two. "I'm sorry, Marc. I can't get past it; the gender thing. I know in my heart it shouldn't matter, but my brain... it kicked into overdrive when we kissed. Maybe we could just be friends. Hang out every once in a while? See another movie together?"

Marc shook his head. "No. I can't do that. I thought maybe I could. But seeing you here today... I wouldn't be able to do it. You and I only spent a few hours together, but you did something to me. From the first moment I saw you, I knew you'd steal my heart, but I was desperately hoping you'd tend it for me."

Good Lord. What incredibly romantic star had this man fallen from?

"So, that's it?" Adam clutched tighter to the railing. "I'm not going to see you again?" The thought made him feel sick to his stomach.

"We might bump into each other." Marc stepped closer, extending his arms for a hug. He dragged Adam into them and clung to him, inhaling the heady scent of Adam's sweat dampened skin. "I think we could've been incredible together." He pulled back and softly kissed Adam's lips. "Goodbye, Adam. Take care of yourself."

Adam's knees practically buckled as he watched Marc climb down the steps and walk away. And then the confusion and regret set in. Was the wall in his mind really that thick? And who the fuck had built the damn thing it in the first place? *Fuck!*

He turned and stumbled back inside. Dancing was the only thing that could soothe him right now.

It was late. Well past midnight. The freshly washed dishes clattered into the sink, making Kelsey jump. She twisted away from the makeshift picnic she and Adam had spread out on her bed, to see if he was alright.

"Sweetheart?"

Adam folded his arms at the edge of the sink and sunk his forehead onto them. "I'm okay, Kelsey."

"No, you're not." Kelsey struggled to her feet. "I've never seen you like this before." She stroked small circles on Adam's back to soothe him. "He really got to you, didn't he?"

"You have no idea."

Digging her chin into Adam's shoulder, Kelsey wrapped her arms around Adam's waist. "Are you in love with him?"

"Christ, Kelsey. I only spent a few hours with the guy."

"That's not what I asked." Kelsey gripped Adam's shoulders and turned him to face her. "I asked you if you were in love with him."

Adam pinched up his face, waves of anguish setting his lips at an odd angle, and slipped his arms around Kelsey's neck. He sunk into Kelsey's shoulder in tears and hugged her to him, willing Kelsey's presence to take away his pain. His intense feelings for Marc were tearing him apart inside, and he had no idea what to do about it. "What am I going to do?"

"Why don't you call him?" Kelsey replied.

"And say what, Kelsey? 'Marc, I think I'm falling in love with you. Please won't you be my friend.'"

"Yeah, actually that would be a good place to start."

Adam turned away from her. "I can't say that."

"Alright, it doesn't have to be that heavy, but you need to tell him how you feel." Kelsey scratched affectionately at the short bristly hairs at the back of Adam's neck. She'd cut his hair for him tonight. "He needs to know how strongly you feel about him."

Adam really didn't want to do this, but the thought of losing Marc, forever, outweighed any thought of listening to the butterflies in his stomach. He dropped down onto the sofa, picked up the phone and listened to the dial tone as he ironed out the folded scrap of paper, Marc had written his cell number on, flat with his hand.

His fingers trembled as he dialled. Slipping and pressing the wrong numbers repeatedly, forcing him to start again. He finally got it right and waited.

"Hello," Marc said. He sounded groggy. Adam almost hung up.

"Hey, it's me."

"Hey, me."

Adam swore he could hear Marc smiling through the phone and his stomach immediately warmed to the sound.

"How was your practice today?" *Idiot. You didn't phone Marc at one in the morning to chit chat about his day.*

"It was alright. It'll be nice when it warms up a bit."

The sound of Marc shifting in bed caught Adam's attention. "I'm sorry for phoning so late. Were you asleep?"

"Trying to." There was a long pause. "I wasn't expecting to hear from you. Is everything alright?"

Adam closed his eyes, setting his confidence. "Yeah, but there's something I need to tell you. Could we talk for a minute?"

Another long pause. "Sure. What's up?"

"Marc… this morning at the studio… when you walked away." Adam stopped, gathering his courage. He needed to say this. "It felt like someone was tearing my guts out. I can't stop thinking about you either. And I can't stand the thought of never seeing you again."

"So, what does that mean exactly?"

Adam ground the heel of his hand into his temple, attempting to relieve the stress. "I need you, Marc. I want us to be together."

"But Adam, if you're hung up on the physical stuff, how are we going to do that?"

"I don't know." Adam ran his hand through his hair, exasperated. "Maybe over time, I could get past it."

"It doesn't work like that, Adam. Either you're attracted to me, physically, or you're not."

"But see, that's the thing. I am. I really am." Adam slid over as Kelsey sat down beside him. He leaned into her as she wrapped a supportive arm around his shoulders. "You wouldn't believe some of the dreams I've been having about you. Seriously 'R' rated stuff."

A soft laugh rolled through the phone. "I don't know, Adam."

"Tell him," Kelsey whispered and Adam shook his head.

"This whole thing with you really did a number on me," Marc continued. "My game has been completely off." He exhaled with uncertainty. "Adam, what if we get into this together, and I fall in love with you? I know I told you I was more interested in you than your cherry, but not being able to touch the person I love... I wouldn't be able to do that."

Adam dropped his head into his hand. He was losing him. This was it. He was going to lose Marc forever. His heart began thrumming out of control in his throat. "Marc please—"

Kelsey jabbed Adam with her elbow and he shook his head more vehemently. He wasn't going to use love as a bargaining chip to get Marc back. That would put undo pressure on him.

"Okay. I'll think about it, Adam. I'm not promising anything, except that I'll think about it."

"That's all I'm asking." Adam let out a sigh of relief. "I'll let you get back to sleep."

"Sure. Goodnight, Adam."

"Goodnight." Adam hung up the phone and collapsed into the cushions. "He's going to think about it."

"Well, that's something at least," Kelsey replied. "Meanwhile, you need to figure out a way to deprogram yourself."

"I know." Adam stretched, feeling much more relaxed. "Maybe I'll talk to some of the guys down at the studio. Find out what I'm potentially getting myself into."

Kelsey snorted in amusement. "I'm not sure if that's a good idea." She smacked Adam on the back as she removed herself from the sofa. "Baby steps young Padawan. Get Marc back first, then figure out what you want to do to him."

"I know exactly what I want to do to him," Adam said as he straightened out his sleeping bag and slipped inside. "I'm more concerned about what he wants to do to me."

"Like I said, Adam. Let's not cross that bridge yet, alright?"

Shoving his shoulder under his pillow, Adam settled in, feeling more hopeful than he had in days. He could do this. If Marc decided to come back to him, he would do anything to keep him.

The sound of a body crashing to the floor broke Adam's attention. Or lack of attention, as the case may be. He spun around to find his prima ballerina sprawled out on the floor at his feet. He'd dropped her again. And she was pissed.

"What the fuck is wrong with you, Adam?" Katarina asked as steamed anger surged her lithe, elegant body to its feet. "It's a simple fucking lift. One that we've done a thousand times before."

"I'm sorry, Kat," Adam replied. "I'm a little distracted."

"Obviously." Katarina dropped her hands onto her hips, and sighed with exasperation. "So, who is she this time?"

"What do you mean?" Adam waved the pianist away. He needed to take a break so he could clear his head. Dropping Kat again was going to cost him his life. He knew all too well. He'd been plagued by Kat's existence since he was sixteen years old. The ballet community was, at times, uncomfortably small, and the likelihood of working with the same people, again and again, guaranteed.

"Don't give me that crap, Casanova." Katarina lifted her shawl off the high barre and draped it around her shoulders. This particular studio they were using for rehearsals was cold and draughty, and required constant covering up each time they took a break.

"How long have we known each other?" Katarina asked.

"Too long, obviously."

"God, Adam. I wish you would find someone and settle down. Properly this time. Every time you go through one of your epic break-ups, it increases my chances of getting broken. Your crazy love life has pretty much ruined your career, you know that, right?"

"I'm well aware of that." Adam stretched out his shoulders. Kat was right. Every time one of his relationships came to a fiery end, he lost his focus, and came off looking far less impressive than what he was capable of. It had cost him more than a few principal roles, and he'd subsequently lost the support of the private backers he'd worked so hard to find. Not ever again. He was done with the whole relationship business. He needed to focus on dance.

Kat touched Adam's arm. "Adam?" She pulled anxiously at the sleeve of his shirt. "Do you know tall, dark and handsome back there?"

Adam spun around. It had been over two weeks since he'd spoken to Marc on the phone, and he'd given up hope that he was ever going to hear from him again. Seeing Marc standing there, waiting for him; Adam was at a loss as to what he was feeling at that moment. His insides felt as if they were melting.

"Hey, stranger," Adam said, gliding towards Marc. His heart jumped in his chest, fluttering, as a grin lit up Marc's face.

"I decided I couldn't stay away after all," Marc said.

"Thank God." Adam bit his bottom lip, restraining a tear that was threatening to escape. "My poor heart couldn't take much more."

Marc stepped closer. "Yeah?"

Adam nodded and let Marc sweep him up, burying his face into the warm curve of Marc's neck. "I'm so sorry. I was such an idiot."

"Hey, it's alright." Marc kissed the top of Adam's head, holding him closer as Adam lost it and broke down. There was no stopping the tears staining his face. The relief Adam felt as he was being held by Marc again was immense.

"I thought I was never going to see you again," Adam said.

"Shh… I'm here now. I'm not going anywhere." Marc raised his gaze and nodded to Katarina in acknowledgment of her presence. She was leaning against the bar, one hand on her hip, waiting. When she started tapping her foot impatiently, Marc decided he needed to peel Adam off his chest to address her. She didn't look like the kind of woman you wanted to tangle with.

"Adam. Maybe you should introduce me," Marc said, turning Adam away from his body. He dug around in his pockets and found a fresh tissue and handed it to Adam.

Adam sniffed wetly, accepting it and dabbed at his eyes. "Marc, this is Katarina Tredyakovsky. Our prima ballerina, and persistent thorn in my side."

Katarina tipped her head, intrigued. "You can call me Kat for short." She posed demurely and waited, not wanting to extend her hand until the introductions were complete. She exhaled softly in irritation when Adam didn't continue.

"I'm Marc Tucker." Marc took Katarina's timidly offered hand. "I'm a friend of Adam's. We met in a class he was teaching."

The incredible arch achieved by Katarina's eyebrow at this statement had Adam clutching his gut in amusement, unable to speak. "You were in one of Adam's classes?" Katarina asked to clarify she'd heard Marc correctly. "You take ballet?"

"Me and some of the guys from my football team—"

Katarina blinked. "That makes more sense." She eyed Adam, who was gradually regaining his sensibilities, and tucked a finger into the corner of her delicate mouth, in feigned consideration.

"So… friends?" she continued, waggling her finger back and forth between the two men. "That's the story you're going with?"

"Yes, Kat," Adam answered. "That's what we're going with."

"Alright." Katarina threw her shawl back onto the barre. "That would certainly explain the funk you've been in." She stepped into the center of the room. "So, Adam. Now that lover boy has returned to your life, could we please get back to work? Perhaps we can complete this lift without you dropping me again."

"You dropped her?" Marc asked in disbelief.

"Yeah. A few times." Adam lowered his voice. "Don't let her delicate frame fool you. That woman is as tough as nails, and could probably take us both out with one hand tied behind her back."

"I heard that," Katarina said.

"I better let you get back to it," Marc said. "I just wanted to see you before I headed out of town again."

Adam reached for the edge of Marc's coat. He'd been entertaining thoughts of them spending the night together. "How long will you be gone for?"

"Four days this time."

"Four days?" Adam slumped against Marc's shoulder, laughing softly. "You're trying to kill me." He looked up into Marc's eyes. "I said I was sorry, didn't I?" He ran his fingers down the front of Marc's shirt, lingering just above his belt. "I want to be with you."

"Fucking hell, Adam." Marc licked his lips, sending a shiver up Adam's spine, and tipped Adam's chin up to softly take his mouth. The warmth of Marc's breath surrounded Adam, taking the creeping chill out of his bones, and he knew without question, he never wanted to leave the security of that place again. He hummed happily against Marc's mouth, savouring it; the voices in his mind, silent at last.

"Adam!"

Adam pulled away from Marc's mouth, glancing over at a scowling Katarina. "I better go, or the dragon lady will come and get me."

"Don't drop her again." Marc snuck a quick kiss. "And phone me when you get home tonight."

"It'll be late."

"I'll wait up."

Tucking a tongue into one cheek, Adam bounced back over to where Katarina was waiting for him. His world was right again.

The phone only rang once before Marc picked up. Adam squirmed on the sofa, ecstatic. Marc had been waiting for his call.

"How was your flight?" Adam asked.

"Tedious."

"I just got in. We had a late rehearsal. Were you asleep?"

"No, I was just watching a movie."

Adam perked up; anxious to find things to talk about. They barely knew each other. Which was kind of weird considering how he felt about Marc. He really didn't know anything about him, other than the fact he played football for a living.

"What movie is it?" Adam asked. "I can't hear it."

Marc chuckled throatily. "I muted it before I answered the phone."

"So, what movie is it?"

"Oh, god, Adam… seriously?"

"Is it a porno?" Adam tucked his feet up onto the sofa, his breath catching with excitement. He suddenly felt like a teenager whispering to some girl on the phone from the relative privacy of his bedroom closet. Except this was no girl. This was a gorgeous, virile man with the ability to bring him shuddering to his knees.

"Yeah," Marc answered.

"Gay porn?"

Marc's voice rumbled as he laughed. "What do you think?"

"Turn the sound back up." Adam shifted on the sofa. His cock was expanding fiercely against the band of his sweats. The prospect of hearing men actually fucking each other was driving his desire in a direction he never would've thought possible until he'd met Marc. He gripped the edge of the sofa, listening with apt attention as the volume of Marc's television increased.

Holy fuck! Adam laughed out a short gasp of air.

"Can you hear alright?" Marc asked.

"Yeah… definitely." Adam slipped his hand inside the front of his sweats and hauled his underwear aside. "What are they doing?"

"Just a second—"

Adam bit his lip in anticipation. He could hear Marc moving around in the hotel room. And then the sound of rustling sheets.

"Okay," Marc said, picking up the phone again. "Door's locked against marauding footballers."

Adding a seductive tone to his voice, Adam whispered into the phone. "So, what are you wearing?" It had the desired effect; Marc cracked up at the other end of the line.

Adam waited for Marc to quieten. "Tell me what they're doing."

"Well, you see it all started when the one guy had a leaky faucet and had to call a plumber, because apparently, when you're hot and hung, you don't have the fortitude to swap out a simple washer."

Adam snorted happily. "Someone sounds pretty pleased with the plumbing service he's receiving."

"Mm… yeah. The plumber. Decent body on him. Easily eight inches… cut. He's got hot and hopeless down on his knees." A sharp exhalation of air. "Fuck!"

"What?" Adam asked as he struggled with his sweats, pulling them off his hips. "What's happening?"

"Hottie isn't so hopeless after all." Marc grunted as he rearranged himself in bed. "The guy can give some pretty serious head."

"Tell me exactly what he's doing." Adam settled in, stroking his cock in long even passes as he listened to Marc relay the details of the scene he was watching. It wasn't so much what the two men were doing that was building Adam up, but the tone of Marc's voice, and the breathy pauses of Marc's mounting arousal.

Adam cradled the handset between his ear and shoulder, spat quietly into his hand and began stroking his cock more earnestly, pulling and twisting the head with each upstroke, the sound of Marc's voice driving him. A groan escaped his lips as he circled his thumb over the slit, spreading the pre-cum around the tip.

"Fuck… Adam… are you?"

"Uh huh… yeah," Adam said softly as he shifted his ass, sliding further down the sofa.

"Are you wet?"

"Dripping…"

"Fuck." Marc's voice dropped seductively. "Stroke it for me."

"Yeah?"

"Yeah… nice, long, easy strokes."

Adam licked his lips. "Mm… that feels good. It's making me so hard." *Christ, I've never been so fucking hard.* "My balls are aching to be touched. Can I touch them?"

"Fuck… Adam." Marc's voice caught in his throat. "Take them in your hand… massage them gently. And real slow."

Manoeuvring the phone so it wouldn't fall away, Adam freed up his other hand and slid it between his legs, dropping them wide open as he fondled his tightening sacs. "Ah… that's nice."

"Are you still stroking your dick?"

"Mm... hm." Adam moaned as a wave of the combined sensation washed over him. "My cock's so hot... and hard." He groaned, picturing Marc with him. "God, Marc, I want you so bad."

The quaking shudder from Marc translated through the phone perfectly, almost setting Adam off. He released his balls and calmed himself, keeping an even, steady rhythm on his dick.

"Adam?"

"Yeah, I'm good. What now?"

"Use your thumb to play with your slit until it's nice and wet, and then run it around the ridge of your head.

"Yeah... that's nice." Adam gasped; he was getting close, and knowing that Marc was listening, was bringing him to the edge much sooner than he'd expected. "I'm close, Marc."

"Okay... start stroking your cock again, faster this time." Marc grunted as he shifted his own position again. "Can you reach your ass?"

Adam's mind blurred. "What?" He examined his free hand. He'd never done that before. He'd been tempted, but—

"Adam?"

"Oh! Fuck!" The addition of his finger was almost too much. Adam's ass clenched tightly around it, drawing it hungrily into his body as his hips bucked up, his balls tensing, ready to release their load.

God, that feels incredible.

"Adam—"

"Fuck! I'm going to cum." It couldn't be helped; the handset of the phone fell to the floor as Adam pumped his cock harder, twisting and pulling, teasing the seed from his balls. Shifting his weight, he thrust his finger further into his ass, seeking the gland he knew was supposed to be there; somewhere. *Fuck, where is it?* He dropped his head back, exasperated. *Some homosexual you're going to make.*

Fuck it. Adam removed his finger and grabbed for the phone, concentrating on what he knew instead. He hocked into his hand and took control of his cock again.

"Marc?"

"Did you cum?"

"Not yet… you?"

Marc groaned and almost dropped his phone. "No, but I'm close."

Adam closed his eyes and imagined that Marc was lying next to him, and they were getting each other off.

Marc's warm, slick hand was on his dick, pulling him to the edge. And his was wrapped around Marc's smooth, hard cock; stroking.…

"I'm cumming," Marc said and grunted through a series of convulsions, exhaling bursts of seductive air through the phone. That was all it took. Adam exploded; streams of thick, wet bursts escaping from his cock, coating his shirt and leaving tiny droplets as far up as his cheek. His body jerked through each surge as he milked every last drop.

"I take it that you and Marc are back together then? Or have you started using a 'phone sex' service?"

Adam spun around. He hadn't heard Kelsey come in.

"Is that Kelsey?" Marc asked through shocks of laughter. "How long has she been standing there?"

"I'm sure she'll tell me," Adam replied as he attempted to wipe his hand clean on his shirt. "She's not shy about stuff like that."

"I can't wait to meet her."

"You say that now." Adam sighed with contentment, swiping the drops of cum from his face. "Well, hopefully that'll hold me until you get back."

"What? You're not going to phone me tomorrow night?"

Adam sat up. "You want me to?"

"I'd pay money to hear those sounds you make when you cum. If you don't phone me, I'll be tempted to skip the rest of my games and hijack a plane, so I can get home to you."

"God, Marc. Are we really doing this? Seeing each other?"

"Are you having second thoughts?"

"No, not at all. I can't wait to feel your arms around me again." Adam smiled when Kelsey launched into an imitation of puking. "And feel your body against mine for the first time." He bit his lip to keep from laughing. Kelsey was practically in hysterics.

Marc's laugh rumbled through the phone. "We'd better call it a night. I need to get some sleep, and it sounds like you're causing your roommate a significant amount of pain."

"She'll live. Me on the other hand… not so sure."

"We'll talk tomorrow?"

"Yeah, I'll call you."

"Alright. Goodnight, Adam."

"Night." Adam hung up the phone. "Love you…"

Kelsey plopped down on the sofa next to him. "Adam?" She touched his arm, tickling his wrist with her fingers. She didn't need to actually ask the question.

"So much it's painful." Adam tucked himself into Kelsey's side. He'd never felt this vulnerable before. His entire world was in someone else's hands, and it scared the shit out of him.

Chapter Four

"Alright," Marc said from the phone in his car. He'd just left the airport parking lot, and was headed for Adam's apartment. "I'll be there in about twenty minutes."

"I can't wait to see you."

"I could barely sleep last night, thinking about getting home to you. I feel like I've known you forever."

Adam's face lit up and then flushed. He still couldn't believe this incredible man wanted him. They'd spent hours on the phone each night, talking about absolutely everything; their childhoods, their friends, their hopes, dreams, beliefs; everything; even their deepest fears. Taking this next step with Marc felt like the most natural thing in the world.

The wait took forever; it seemed much longer than twenty minutes. When the phone rang for the front door, Adam jumped, almost knocking the handset off the cradle.

"I have to come down to let you in," Adam said over the intercom. "The number seven button doesn't work on this phone."

"Okay, but hurry."

Adam rushed down the stairs, threw open the door, and immediately leapt into Marc's arms. His voice squeaked with surprise when Marc hoisted him up off the ground and backed him up against a wall, forcing Adam to wrap his legs around Marc's waist. He melted into Marc's warm and tentative kiss, and it made his head spin; in a good way. A very good way.

"How was your flight?" Adam asked nonchalantly, as if he weren't hanging from the neck of the most gorgeous man he'd ever laid eyes on. And their cocks weren't brushing against each other. And their lips weren't still touching; and Marc's warm breath wasn't rolling across his tongue.

"It was the longest flight ever." Marc brushed his lips back and forth across Adam's. "I could've run home faster."

"Then you would've been too tired by the time you got here."

A smile stretched across Marc's face, and he set Adam back down on his feet. "Let's go upstairs."

Adam clutched Marc's hand, comforted by its strength and growing familiarity as he followed Marc up the stairs, and watched the smooth movement of Marc's muscles beneath his clothes. His dick twitched at the sight of Marc's ass in front of him, and he felt a sharp twinge of pain radiate up into his own, followed by a sense of longing. He'd never experienced anything like that before; that type of longing, and it frightened him. Was this really what he wanted?

He opened the door of the apartment and stumbled through, with Marc heavy on his heels. The air was practically knocked out of him as Marc pressed him up against the wall, shoved the door closed with his foot, and chased after his mouth, enveloping it, and penetrating its warmth. Marc's tongue surged and sparred as he sought out Adam's desire. And it was there; heated and urgent.

Yes, Marc… please… I want to be with you… so much.

Suddenly thrown into turmoil, Adam's heart shuddered. It was too much. It felt too good. Marc's tongue was probing and tasting, and doing incredible things to his senses, but his mind had sprung to life and it was clouding his head with noise; objecting profusely. Panic welled up into his chest, spreading to his limbs—

"Stop!" Adam ducked his face away and struggled under Marc's assault, grasping at the wall behind him to try and pull away, but Marc held him firmly in place, only backing off enough to speak.

"Shh… Adam. You're alright. I've got you."

Adam looked up into Marc's eyes. They were warm and comforting, and held his gaze with such affection. He wanted to be held by this man more than he wanted to take his next breath.

"I'm sorry, Marc," he said. "I'm freaking out a little. You have no idea how hard this is for me."

Marc rested his forehead against Adam's. "I know you're scared." He exhaled softly across Adam's lips, sending Adam's heart racing. "Are you sure you want to do this with me?"

Adam removed his hands from the wall behind and gripped Marc's shoulders instead. They felt sturdy and safe. "I've never felt this way about anyone before." He brushed his thumbs across them, drawing strength from them. "I want this to work between us more than you can possibly imagine."

"Then we'll work through this together." Marc tipped Adam's face up so he could look into his eyes. "Remember? We talked about this. You're not alone. I'm right here with you, alright?"

Adam sighed as some of the tension was released from his chest. Marc was right. They could work through this as a couple. *He and Marc together, as a couple. Yeah, that's definitely what he wanted.* He nodded his head and snuck a quick kiss of Marc's lips.

"Good," Marc said as he traced his fingers across Adam's eyebrows, smoothing them. "But maybe we should just hang out tonight, and leave this heavier stuff for another time."

"No—" Adam gripped Marc's shoulders tighter. "I want this. I want to feel you holding me." His breath slowed and escaped full and heavy. "I need you, Marc."

Breathing deeply, with Marc's assistance, Adam steadied his heart rate and relaxed against the wall as Marc took his mouth again, and willed his mind to be silent. His confidence soared and his cock hardened, rapidly and undeterred as Marc shifted closer to him, breathing much heavier now; emboldening Adam to let his body take over and sink fully into Marc's warm, welcoming mouth; taking everything it was offering. And it was offering freedom. Freedom from the wall of denial he'd allowed the construction of; a wall that had been erected by a combination of upbringing and fear. Not everyday fear, but fear of eternal damnation; an eternity of pain and suffering in the flames. Homosexuality was a sin. He was going to hell; without question. He'd been taught that in church from the time he was old enough to understand what sex was.

Leviticus 20:13 - "If a man lies with a man as one lies with a woman, both of them have done what is detestable. They must be put to death; their blood will be on their own heads." Adam wrapped his arms tighter around Marc's body, stroking his strong back and running his hands up into Marc's hair; enjoying the feel and taste of him, and knowing, in his heart, that this was meant to be. How could something that felt so right, be so wrong?

1 John 4:7 - "Beloved, let us love one another, for love is from God, and whoever loves has been born of God and knows God."

Was it truly love he felt for Marc? Or was it simply carnal temptation? Were his feelings for Marc rooted in anything other than physical attraction?

Marc moaned eagerly, his desire mounting, sending shivers to Adam's core for many reasons. He realized at that moment, it wasn't just about what his body wanted. He wanted it. His intellectual brain wanted a relationship with this man; a deep, meaningful, loving, and maybe even lifelong relationship. Premature as his feelings of love for Marc were, they couldn't be wrong. Wanting to spend the rest of his life with someone; that would be love in its purest form. And his mother had always told him, God was love.

"I can hear your mind spinning," Marc commented playfully.

"There's a serious demolition job going on inside my head right now." Adam tried to laugh, but it came out as a weak, panicked exhalation. His heart was hammering relentlessly against his lungs.

"Do you want to stop for a minute, so you can clear away some of the debris?"

"No, I'm alright." Adam closed his eyes, thinking back to his childhood and the hours upon hours he'd spent in church with his mother. "It's amazing how something told to me as a child could shape my life so dramatically."

"Children believe what they hear, Adam, especially when it comes from their parents."

Adam heaved a sigh of regret. He'd left his son, Connor, to the rigid teachings of his ex-wife and her parents. He just hoped his son wasn't gay. *God, how can you say that?*

Marc brushed a hand through Adam's hair to catch his attention. "Hey, are you still with me?"

"Yeah… sorry." Adam reached up and touched Marc's lips with his fingers, marvelling at their warmth.

"Adam, do you trust me?"

"Yeah." Adam nodded his head. "Of course I do."

"Good." Marc deftly undid the buttons of Adam's shirt and let it slip from Adam's shoulders, pooling onto the floor. "We're going to take this slow, alright? If you need me to stop, you just let me know." He brushed his lips across Adam's. "I'll stop, without a single question or judgment. I promise."

"I know you will." Adam held his breath as Marc's lips traced down the side of his neck and across his shoulder; leaving open mouth kisses in its wake. And it really was a wake, because it was leaving Adam's body trembling violently. He bit his lip, tipping his head back against the wall, and moaned softly as Marc's tongue circled a nipple and then sucked it into his mouth, pulling on it gently. None of the women he'd been with had ever given his nipples any attention, but Marc was sucking and licking at them with an ardent desire that was thrilling Adam straight through to his toes. He'd never considered they'd be so sensitive. His body tensed.

Oh, my God! An unexpected warmth of untamed desire rushed eagerly to Adam's cock, causing it to strain against the thread bare, pajama bottoms he was wearing, tenting them awkwardly. *Oh, fuck... Marc's hand.* It was travelling up Adam's inner thigh and was soon rubbing Adam's cock into a state of fervid attention.

Adam's breath caught, his panic mounting, as Marc abandoned his nipples to lick a line down the center of his body. Licking and devouring; tasting everything. He felt the string of his pyjama bottoms loosen, and then they fell to the floor, exposing him completely; he hadn't bothered pulling on any underwear after Marc phoned, thinking they'd be a hindrance.

Christ. The cool air brushed across his thighs and his stiff, leaking cock, which was now protruding fiercely from his body. *I can't believe I'm doing this.* His anxiety must've been evident in his breathing, because Marc was suddenly up at his mouth again.

"Are you alright?" Marc asked between delicate licks of Adam's lips and then tiny nips at his chin.

"I'm fine." Adam stroked Marc's face with his hand. It was the first time he'd touched Marc's face like this. The stubble felt strange, but comforting; normal. "Keep going. It feels really good."

"Yeah?" Marc bit playfully at Adam's lip and pressed his hips against Adam's, pinning him tighter to the wall, and thrusting his own hard dick against Adam's stomach through the thick material of his jeans. Adam groaned and ground back against Marc, tempting him to take Adam's mouth again; more passionately this time; breathing in the sounds Adam was making.

"I love those sounds you make when you're turned on," Marc said as he abandoned Adam's mouth. "Makes me want to cover you in syrup and eat you." He grinned as Adam coughed out a laugh. "Yeah, I thought so."

"Was I that obvious?"

"You were practically drooling." Marc winked in response to Adam's stunned expression, and then licked and kissed his way back down Adam's body, circling each of Adam's nipples first. He stopped at the thin trail of hair that would fan out around Adam's cock, enjoying the feel of the hardened member brushing against his cheek, and wanting to savour the heat radiating from Adam's body. He also wanted to give Adam a moment to adjust.

Adam gazed down at Marc, crouched in front of him serenely enjoying the closeness, and his tightly wound feelings for Marc swelled exponentially, spilling everywhere; and he didn't care if they did. It felt incredible. He'd never felt so alive.

He brushed his hand through Marc's hair, causing Marc to look up. Those eyes. That face. That incredibly beautiful, caring and sensitive man. He wanted all of it, and he felt at peace with his decision. Being in love, for the very first time in his life, meant more to him than any promise of salvation ever had.

"Hey, you," Adam said.

"Hey—" Marc smiled up at him and rubbed his cheek against Adam's cock and then turned his face enough to run a tentative tongue along its length while keeping an eye on Adam's reaction. Emboldened by Adam's acceptance, Marc shifted his weight and lowered himself onto his knees, and took Adam's shaft into his hand, stroking it in slow even strokes as a spool of pre-cum collected and then stretched out towards the floor. Marc caught the strand with his tongue and returned it to its source, taking the velvety head of Adam's dick between his lips.

Even a preconceived notion of keeping his voice down would've been pointless. Adam was vocal. He couldn't help it. And the things Marc was doing with his mouth and tongue were beyond any possibility of audio temperance.

"Fuck yeah—" Adam groaned, gripping the wall for support. Marc's mouth felt nothing like a woman's. There was incredible strength pulling at his cock; incredible strength and a desperate primal hunger. A hunger he could understand. A hunger he'd felt burning within him, but never knew what to do with. Now he knew. He and Marc; they could feed off each other.

"Do you want to head over to the bed?" Adam suggested, pulling Marc to his feet.

"Will Kelsey mind?"

"I always sleep on her bed when she's not here."

Marc caught Adam's gaze, studying him for any lingering apprehension. "I wasn't planning on doing any sleeping."

The corner of Adam's mouth twitched and his dick jerked against the flat of his stomach. He'd never wanted anyone as desperately as he wanted Marc. The desire he felt was unfamiliar. Unfamiliar and wonderful. He took Marc's hand, led him over to the bed and proceeded to remove Marc's shirt for him.

"I should hope not," Adam replied. "If you fall asleep on me you're going to be in trouble."

Marc snorted out a soft laugh. "Not going to happen. Lay down for me," he said, taking his shirt from Adam's hand and tossing it onto the floor. "I want to look at you."

Adam complied, stretching out on the mattress, self conscious of the fact he was completely naked in front of the man that wanted him; wanted his body. And that he was going to be giving it to him.

"Fuck… Adam. Your body is incredible."

Adam's face flushed. "Take your clothes off," he said as his gaze roamed across Marc's chest; it was broad and muscular, and Marc's nipples were thick, dark, and so damn lickable. He sat up expectantly; his cock now leaking profusely against his stomach.

God, Adam, you are so completely gay. Moron.

Marc's hands shifted towards his belt, undoing it and then the button and fly of his jeans. He wasn't wearing underwear either, and Adam caught his first glimpse of the rock hard cock he was to become intimately familiar with; his breath caught. It was long and thick, and absolutely fucking gorgeous. *Yeah, you're definitely gay.*

Adam swallowed the pool of saliva that was collecting in his mouth, and licked his lips; his eyes transfixed on Marc's cock. He was stunned by how much he wanted it; how much he wanted the swollen head of Marc's dick gracing his lips and wet, anxious surface of his tongue; and how much he needed to taste it.

"Come here," Adam said, raising up onto his knees and grasping Marc's thighs to bring him closer. He slipped a hand under Marc's balls and lifted them, letting them rest in the palm of his hand. They were cool and heavy against his fingers. Adam shuffled closer, inhaling the scent pervading the crease of Marc's groin, and ran his tongue along the base of Marc's stiff, tight cock, letting the heated softness of Marc's shaft grace his cheek. He tipped his face into it, stroking its length with his lips.

That feels incredible.

He dropped back, so he could see the glistening moisture of Marc's arousal, and pressed his thumb into the slit to collect the pre-cum. He smeared it right back to the ridge of Marc's cock head and his gut clenched; the feel of the slick surface drawing him closer. Marc moaned and thrust his hips forward as Adam's tongue cleaned the head off and dipped into the wet.

Tastes so good...

Taking more of Marc's dick into his mouth, Adam attempted to close his lips around it to ensure some suction as the velvety helmet graced the roof of his mouth.

I need more.

Adam rose up higher onto his knees and allowed the entire shaft to enter his mouth. He gagged awkwardly, embarrassment colouring his cheeks, but relaxed fully as Marc's hand affectionately brushed the top of his head;

allowing the heavy cock full access to his throat. The coarse hairs tickled his nose as he began to bob up and down on Marc's dick.

Fuck, I love this. The taste of it. The feel of it running past my lips and tongue. Filling my mouth. Stroking my throat.

Adam looked up. Marc was making the most incredible sounds of arousal. He needed to see Marc's face.

Fuck, he's even more gorgeous when he's like this.

"Mm…" Marc groaned, brushing a thumb across Adam's cheek. "Pull down hard on my balls." He grunted and tipped his head back as Adam complied. "Harder… fuck—" He clutched at Adam's shoulder. "That's it… I'm going to cum—"

Adam pulled his mouth off Marc's cock and took over with his hand, pumping the thick shaft with increasing intensity as he licked at the head. He wanted to be close without actually committing himself to having Marc's dick in his mouth when Marc came. He wasn't sure he was ready for that yet.

"Fuck!" Marc's cock hardened, pulsed and jumped in Adam's hand, and the first burst of warm, salty liquid caught Adam by surprise as it surged across his lips and chin, coating them. He licked his lips as he brought his mouth closer for the next pulse, catching most of it on his tongue, and then he capped the head of Marc's dick with his mouth, intent on swallowing the rest.

Adam decided he wanted it; all of it. It was Marc's, and he'd been the one to coax it from Marc's body. He wanted every last drop. He struggled to keep up as Marc pumped more and more seed down his throat. It felt glorious as it trickled into his gut, filling him. He wanted more; so much more. He groaned in despair as the last convulsion rocked through Marc's body.

Marc dropped to his knees on the mattress and pushed Adam over, urgently devouring his mouth. The combined taste of Marc's saliva and cum tumbling across Adam's tongue forced Adam's hips up, desperate to grind heavier against Marc's body. He groaned, satisfied, as Marc allowed more of his weight to press Adam further into the mattress.

"What do you want to do?" Marc asked, his hips now thrusting with purpose against Adam's. A look of panic must've flashed across Adam's expression, because Marc slowed down a bit and kissed Adam gently on the lips. "If you want, we can just keep going like this." He grinned. "I'm pretty sure I can get you off without any added complexities." To prove his point, Marc increased the ferocity of his hips, sending Adam's mind reeling.

"God, that feels good." Adam closed his eyes, enjoying the sensation. They fluttered open a mere second later, and his breath caught; his arousal surging. Marc was hard again, and his thick cock was jamming into Adam's stomach, fighting for a place alongside his own fiercely hard dick. His hands, of their own accord, drifted down Marc's back and grasped desperately at Marc's ass as he wrapped his legs around Marc's body, hauling him closer.

"I'm going to cum," Adam whispered.

Marc responded with a shuddering breath and capped his mouth over Adam's open one, wanting to absorb the sound. His body quaked as Adam released the first grunting 'Fuck', and Marc's own cock responded, releasing its load into the warm, slick space between their bodies. They ground against each other, grasping and swearing; sharing something they could both understand.

Adam ran his hands up into Marc's hair and lowered Marc's face towards him, so he could kiss him. That hadn't felt strange at all. He felt far more comfortable with Marc than he had with either of his wives. Sex with them had felt strained and mechanical. He stroked Marc's face as he gazed up into his eyes. With Marc, his body had felt fluid; alive; connected. He kissed him again.

Chapter Five

"So, that's it?" Kelsey asked, slamming the ketchup down on the full length counter of the diner Adam had agreed to meet her at; a lapse in judgment he was now regretting. At this point, the entire kitchen staff knew what he'd been up to the night before. Kelsey's nickname in college, amongst other things, had been 'Megaphone Annie'. "You just sucked him off," she continued. "And did the whole 'frottage' thing, and nothing else?"

"That was a big step for me, Kelsey." Adam snuck his hand onto Kelsey's plate and stole a few fries, swiping them through the ketchup on the way to his mouth. "If someone had told me a few weeks ago that I'd be sitting here with you today, discussing how incredible sucking some guy's cock was, I'd have knocked them upside the head."

"True." Kelsey swirled her finger through the mountain of ketchup on her plate and tucked it into her mouth. "So, when do you see this gorgeous lover of yours next?"

"Tonight." Adam reached down the counter and grabbed a stack of napkins. Kelsey was the most disgusting eater he'd ever come across. To her, everything was finger food. He handed her a napkin to clean her hands. "He has a game tonight. I'm going to watch him play and then we're heading back to his place for dinner."

Kelsey snorted. "You mean dessert."

Adam ignored her.

"What time is it?" he asked.

"When are you going to get your own damn cell phone?" Kelsey pulled hers from her pocket. "It's just after four."

"I need to get going." Adam gathered up his jacket and the leather gloves he'd picked up at the thrift store. Kelsey was going to kill him when she found out he'd spent most of his pay cheque on clothes, but tonight was important. He was going to be meeting the rest of Marc's team, and their wives, and he didn't want to embarrass Marc by looking like a homeless person.

Kelsey bit her bottom lip in admiration. "You look nice, Adam."

"I picked up a couple of things today." Adam looked down at himself. "Just some decent slacks and a dress shirt."

"You clean up real good, sweetheart. Marc's a lucky guy."

"Thanks, Kelsey." Adam leaned down and gave Kelsey a wet, sloppy kiss on the cheek, grinning as she shoved him away and frantically wiped at it with a napkin.

"God, Adam… that's disgusting."

"Payback for the snowball." Adam winked at her and headed for the door. "Don't wait up."

Adam leaned against the wall of the stadium, shivering. Marc had said he'd meet him outside the back doors at four thirty, but Adam wasn't sure what time he'd actually arrived. Maybe he'd been late? He was certain, though, that he'd been standing there for at least twenty minutes.

Maybe he forgot I was coming.

He jumped as the massive metal door flung open.

"God, there you are," Marc said, pulling Adam into his arms. "I've been looking everywhere for you."

"You said the back doors."

"I'm sorry… I should've been more specific." Marc gripped Adam's face and kissed him. "You're frozen." Bundling Adam inside, Marc laid another kiss on Adam's head. "I meant the back doors down on the north side of the building. I didn't even know these doors were here."

"I'll be fine once you find me some hot chocolate or something."

"Done. There's a dispenser up in the box."

Marc led the way up a few ramps and then used a key to call an elevator that opened up onto a vast hallway with a series of doors down one side. There were lots of people coming and going from the open doorways, briefly chatting with each other and heading off in different directions. Adam recognized some of the guys from the team; they were busy giving their wives kisses, and then running off down the hallway.

"I don't have time to introduce you to everyone right now," Marc said. "I have to get downstairs." He brushed a thumb across the top of Adam's ear. "Will you be alright on your own?"

Adam slipped his fingers down the front of Marc's shirt "I'll be fine… I'll see you after the game."

Marc looked around behind him; most of the people were finding their way back to their boxes in anticipation of the game starting. He bit his lip, preparing to be scandalous, regardless of the backlash, and pushed Adam up against the wall, attacking his mouth in short desperate mouthfuls.

Adam's knees trembled at the intensity of Marc's demands.

"I missed you so much today," Marc said.

"Me too."

"You look incredible… so hot."

"Fuck… Marc."

"Mm… I can't wait to get you home tonight."

Adam tried to steady his breathing, but Marc was pressing him to the wall again, sucking and licking at his neck, and taking away his ability to think clearly. He gasped, clutching at Marc's shoulders. "God, Marc… I love you… so much."

Panic. Adam's heart twisted as Marc released him and backed away. "I'm sorry," Adam stammered. "It just slipped out." He reached for Marc's hand, but Marc stepped back, shaking his head.

"When?" Marc asked; his voice barely above a whisper.

"When what?"

"When did you know?"

"I don't know." Adam scoured his mind. "I started having feelings for you that first day, when you slid that pancake onto my plate." He stepped forward, but Marc tripped out of his reach. Adam's knees really were going to buckle now. His entire universe was collapsing in on itself and there was nothing he could do to stop it.

Marc scrubbed his hand across his face. "We'll talk about this after the game." Both his hands went up and he rubbed furiously at his hair. "I can't get into this with you right now." He shook his head and turned to leave. "I have to go."

Adam stood in stunned silence as he watched Marc race down the long hallway and out of sight. He'd fucked up. Everything had been going perfectly, and he'd fucked it up. He sunk onto the floor.

"Excuse me, sir. You can't sit there."

"Sorry." Adam struggled to his feet, nodding his acknowledgment to the security officer. "I was just leaving anyways." He wiped the back of his hand across his face, smearing the mess of tears already coating his cheeks, and checked along the hallway; not sure what the quickest way out was. He just needed to find an exit before he lost it completely.

The loud hammering on his door became too much to ignore any longer. Marc knew exactly who it was too.

Kelsey had been calling up from the panel outside his apartment building for the past two hours, shrieking at him to let her in. He'd told her to 'go away and mind her own business', but she wasn't hearing any of it.

And now, obviously, someone had let her in.

Marc flung open the door and spun back towards the living room with Kelsey hot on his ass.

"What the fuck is your problem?" Kelsey screamed. "Do you have any idea what you've done to him?"

Marc dropped down onto the sofa and brushed his knuckles across his lips. "I don't know what you want me to say."

"You can start by telling me… what the fuck is your problem?" Kelsey snapped her gum and threw herself down on the coffee table directly in front of Marc.

"Again… don't know what to say." Marc moved to get up, but Kelsey pushed him back into his seat.

"Oh, no you don't. You cannot waltz into my best friend's life like that, steal his heart, utterly destroy him, and then just run away."

"I'm not running away." Marc moved to get up again, but Kelsey shoved him back onto the sofa and held him there. Her hand placed firmly on his chest.

"Well, you're certainly not 'running to'. You haven't called him in three days." Kelsey held up three fingers very close to Marc's face. "Three days... count them. One. Two. Three. Three days." She released Marc's chest and used her hand to smack him in the side of the head.

"Ow... fuck!" Marc lifted a hand to his face where she'd hit him.

Kelsey crossed her arms. "Spill."

"Spill what?"

"Who hurt you?"

"No one hurt me." Marc shielded his face and pushed past Kelsey, headed for the kitchen. He removed a glass from the cupboard and set it on the counter, filling it halfway with orange juice. "Except you, when you smacked me."

"You deserved it. You're an idiot. And idiots deserve to be smacked upside the head."

Adam hadn't been exaggerating about Kelsey, Marc thought. "Look, Kelsey, I don't know how much Adam told you, but..."

"Adam told me everything. He told me that when he confessed his love for you, you pushed him away and bolted... and that it felt like someone was tearing his soul out of his body with their bare hands. That's what he told me."

Marc dropped his head into his hand. "Oh, my God…"

"Yes, exactly… oh, my 'God'. Do you have any idea what Adam was willing to sacrifice to be with you?"

Marc closed his eyes.

"His entire fucking salvation, that's what!" Kelsey struggled out of her coat and chucked it at the sofa, and stormed towards the kitchen. "And you knew that! He told you how fucked up he was about shit like that! And you told him you'd be there for him! That he wouldn't be alone! So, you can understand why, Marc, why, I'm on the verge of ripping your fucking head off, unless you've got a damn good explanation!"

Marc set the glass down. "My last boyfriend had BPD."

"That's what this is about?" Kelsey laughed sharply. "You think Adam has borderline personality disorder?" She set her hand on her hip, breathing heavily, and then relaxed. "Tell me what happened... with this boyfriend of yours."

Marc shifted his posture, confused by Kelsey's sudden change in attack strategy. "It started off normal enough." He shrugged. "Really nice guy… Lawrence. I met him at the gym I was going to." He tapped at the counter, remembering. "After the second date, he was feeling pretty comfortable. Making plans for us to go out again, sending me texts with little hearts."

"You didn't think that was strange?"

"Looking back, yeah, but at the time I just thought it was cute."

"So, when did things change?"

Marc studied Kelsey's face. Her entire countenance had changed. "About three weeks in… Lawrence saw me talking to one of the personal trainers at the gym. I was just setting up my next appointment with the guy."

"Did Lawrence flip out?"

"Yeah, they had to call security. Lawrence was screaming and chucking stuff around, saying that I was a lying, cheating, mother fucker… and I could rot in hell—" Marc sunk down onto one of the stools lining the island in the middle of his kitchen, and began fidgeting with the flower arrangement at its center. "He showed up at my apartment the next day with groceries… to make me dinner; like nothing had happened."

"Did you tell him you didn't want to see him anymore?"

"Yeah, but he wouldn't listen. It was like talking to a seriously freaky broken record. I'd tell him we were through... and the next day he'd be phoning, trying to set up a movie date or something... like we were back together... and it went on like that every fucking day."

"How bad did it get?"

Marc shook his head. "I had to change gyms, sell my condo... move, get an unlisted phone number—"

"So, what makes you think Adam is like Lawrence?"

"Because everything happened so fast with Adam." Marc scrubbed his lips. "And he was willing to give up so much. He'd never even been with a guy before I came along."

Kelsey exhaled noisily. "That's because the right guy hadn't come along. Not because he has a mental illness."

"But some of the things he's told me about his past?"

"No." Kelsey shook her head.

"How can you be so sure?"

"Because I'm a trained psychologist, Marc. I haven't practiced in years, but I can spot a crazy person when I see one... and Adam isn't one of them. I've known Adam for sixteen years. He's in love. That's it. For the first time in his life, Adam O'Neill fell in love, and you were damned lucky to be the one he fell in love with."

Marc's face paled and he closed his eyes. "I have so completely fucked this up, haven't I?"

"Why? Do you have feelings for Adam?"

Marc shook his head. "You're going to laugh at me."

"Try me."

"Fuck—" Marc opened his eyes and laughed.

Kelsey stepped closer and shoved Marc in the shoulder, almost throwing him off balance. "You're in love with him, aren't you?"

"That's a distinct possibility." Marc held up his arms to defend himself against Kelsey's hand as it tried to smack him again.

Kelsey finally snuck one in.

"Ow… fuck! You're a freakin' lunatic, woman."

"See, you're not such an idiot after all." Kelsey retrieved her coat and slipped it back on. "He's down at the studio." She pointed a fierce finger at him. "Don't make me hunt you down again."

The cold dampness was beginning to creep in. The heat had clicked off about an hour ago and the sunlight was fading. It wouldn't be long until he'd have to pack it in for the day. One more time through, Adam thought, and then he'd treat himself to a Chai Latte at the little coffee shop down the street. Maybe even a pumpkin muffin, if they had any left. He deserved something special after getting his heart stomped on. He might even throw dietary caution to the wind and go for something decadent, like a nanaimo bar, or a tuxedo slice, or a thick fudge brownie.

Adam set his starting pose, waiting for the music to begin, and launched into a routine he could probably do in his sleep. The part of Romeo wasn't one of his favorites, but it suited his mood. His life felt like a tragic love story right now; one that he wouldn't be recovering from anytime soon. He was approaching the end of the music when a glimpse of movement caught his eye, but it was so dark in the studio already, he couldn't make out who it was.

Fuck... that's just great. Heartbroken one day, killed the next.

He brushed his hands down his thighs; his bare thighs.

Kind of thought I locked the door.

Over the years, Adam had rehearsed with a few troupes that tended to leave their leotards at the door, and he found he preferred it; especially if he was alone. It brought him the unencumbered sense of freedom he so enjoyed. But standing there naked, in the middle of a dark studio, with someone lurking in the shadows; Adam was craving shackles.

"Who's there?" Adam moved towards the piano and lifted his cane as he peered into the darkness. *What are you going to do? Cane your attacker to death?*

"Fuck," he whispered. The damn light switches were exactly where he'd detected the movement.

"I've never seen you dance before," a soft voice said.

"Marc?" Adam let the cane fall to his side as Marc moved away from the wall and started walking towards him.

"I've never seen anything so beautiful in my life." Marc fell to his knees and wiped the wetness from his cheeks.

"Christ, Marc...." Adam covered the rest of the distance to where Marc was kneeling. "Are you alright?" He frantically pressed the back of his hand against Marc's forehead and felt around his neck, checking for a fever. Marc collapsed the rest of the way, sinking onto his heels and closed his eyes.

"When you were doing that thing," Marc said. "Those leaps around the outside of the room... like you were flying. I thought my heart was going to stop."

Adam knelt down in front of Marc. "Those are called grand jetés, and I kind of threw them in out of boredom." He rubbed his knuckles across Marc's knee. "Don't tell Juliet… she'll be pissed."

Marc opened his eyes again. "I'm sorry."

"Sorry for scaring me half to death… you should be."

"No, I'm sorry for taking off on you the other day. When you told me you loved me, I panicked, and I shouldn't have, because, honestly, I have never felt closer to anyone in my life. It took Kelsey beating me around the head to make me realize that."

Adam pinched his lips together. Kelsey had threatened to go over to Marc's, but he hadn't actually believed she'd do it.

"So, you met Kelsey," he said.

"Yeah, she's a fierce woman," Marc replied. "She loves you a lot. You're lucky to have her on your side."

"A fact I am reminded of on a daily basis." Adam brushed a hand up and down his own arm. "Do you mind if I put some clothes on? It's freezing in here."

Marc reached for Adam's arm as Adam moved to get up.

"Adam, I'm sorry."

Adam pulled his arm away and stood up. "You said that already." He strode back across the room and rummaged his sweatpants out of his bag, hauling them on along with a warm sweater and thick woollen socks. He pulled his boots on.

Marc watched him, cautiously optimistic.

"So, are you going to take me home, or what?" Adam said, throwing his bag over his shoulder.

"Only if it's with me."

"Of course it's with you… you're driving."

"No. I mean, go home, with me... permanently."

Adam crossed his arms over his chest. "You want me to move in with you. After what you put me through. You want me to just forgive you and move in with you."

"Yes."

Exhaling heavily through his nose, Adam wiped a collection of tears away from the corners of his eyes.

Fuck, Marc… I don't know.

Marc stood up. "Adam… please. I love you."

A string of snot ran from Adam's nose and down his lip, making him laugh as he attempted to contain it on his sleeve. "Are you sure, because I'm a bit of a charity case? I may have simply appealed to your benevolent side."

Adam shrieked with joy as Marc rushed at him, hoisted him off the ground and spun him into his arms, and continued spinning until Adam felt like he was going to be sick.

"Alright, alright," Adam said finally. "I'll move in with you." Not wanting to let go, Adam dropped his bag and wrapped his arms around Marc's neck and his legs up around Marc's waist.

"Did you mean it?" Adam asked.

"What?"

"That you love me."

"Of course I did." Marc snuck a quick kiss, but held back; wanting to say everything he was feeling. "I said it before. You're a powerful man, Adam. Powerful and passionate... and a little bit quirky." He grinned. "All good stuff." He brushed his lips across Adam's, soaking in the warmth of his breath. "And you're the most beautiful thing I've ever laid eyes on."

Adam blushed. "I love when you say that." He allowed his feet to slide back onto the floor. "Now take me home. This danseur's body is aching, and needs the attention of a star 'tight end'."

Chapter Six

Adam settled himself against the pillow. It had only taken him twenty minutes to gather up all his belongings from Kelsey's; which was a little embarrassing now that he'd finally seen Marc's place. Marc had told him he didn't get paid much playing for a Canadian football team, but apparently, Marc's birth mother had left him a significant sum of money in her will which Marc had used to buy his first condo before he'd even turned twenty, and the real estate market had been kind to Marc ever since. The two storey studio penthouse had floor to ceiling windows along one wall, offering breathtaking views of the city from the entire space including the loft area where the bed was located.

"Can I get you anything else?" Marc asked as he leaned against the edge of the massive four poster bed.

"No, the chamomile tea is fine, thank you." Adam glanced over at the delicate china teacup sitting on the bedside table next to him. He hadn't actually touched any of it. His stomach was in knots.

What if this is a mistake?

"It's not," Marc said, sinking onto the bed beside him. "Something brought us together, Adam. We never would've run into each other on the street. And even if we had, you wouldn't have given me a second look."

Adam smiled. "Don't be so sure about that."

"I *am* sure about that."

Marc was right. He would've looked, admired and moved on. Telling himself the same lies he'd been telling himself for years. He wasn't interested in guys. He was just more comfortable around them.... And he liked the way they moved.

Lunatic.

Marc reached for Adam's hand. "So, I'm curious." He smirked with a shyness Adam found adorable. "Do you always practice in the nude?"

"When I'm alone, I tend to rehearse that way, yes." Adam lifted the teacup, deciding his stomach was going to be alright after all. "I danced with a troupe based out of Montreal a few years ago that practices almost entirely in the nude. I found I liked it, so I've kept it up. Why do you ask?"

"I was thinking of donating my dining room suite to charity."

Adam snorted into his tea. "What?"

"And replacing the ceramic tiles in the dining room with reclaimed hardwood floors." Marc raised his arm dramatically and fanned it out in front of him. "And then I'd put mirrors down one side, near the kitchen… and a barre down the other."

Adam set his teacup down and fell over, laughing. He reached for Marc, grasping his leg. "That would be really nice, actually."

"Done." Marc crawled closer. "But only if you promise to leave all your leggings and… whatever, back at the studio."

"I have to bring them home to wash them." Adam licked his lips as Marc hovered very close to his mouth.

"I'll have a laundry service pick them up."

Adam extended his tongue and delicately tickled Marc's bottom lip, thrilling in the taste. "What if my tights need darned?"

"I'll buy you new ones."

Adam shivered with excitement. "What if I get cold?"

"Then I'll just have to heat you up." Marc dove at Adam, shoving him into the plush bedding and straddled his body as his tongue slipped between the soft open lips of Adam's mouth.

Adam ran his hands into the legs of Marc's boxer shorts, massaging his thighs and trying to push past Marc's hips, digging his thumbs into the crease of Marc's groin.

"Mm… take these off," Adam said after peeling his lips away from Marc's mouth. He cuddled into the bedding to watch as Marc lifted himself off the bed and stripped away his clothes, leaving Adam utterly speechless.

God, he's beautiful.

Adam sat up and reached for Marc, brushing his fingers up Marc's chest and furrowing them through the dark hairs. Marc sat down on the edge of the bed and cast his gaze downward.

"Adam.…" Marc hesitated, allowing his hand to travel up and down Adam's leg. "This isn't a mistake; you moving in here with me." He looked up, catching Adam's attention and then held it as the emotion built inside him. "I know we haven't known each other for very long, but—"

Adam stopped Marc from continuing by placing a hand on his arm. He knew what Marc was trying to say. Something intense had sparked between them from the very first day they'd met in the studio, and for him, personally, that meant all the years of comfortably wearing the clothes of an arrogant, self-centered prick had just fallen away, leaving him feeling exposed and vulnerable.

And it felt really, really good.

The corners of Adam's mouth turned up; a smile bursting across his face. He was in love with an incredibly beautiful, caring and powerful man, and it felt really, really, fucking amazing.

Really fucking amazing.

"Marc… shh." Adam touched a finger to Marc's lips. "We can talk later. Right now… I want you to make love to me." He leaned in, kissing Marc's lips softly at first, and then he deepened the kiss, drawing Marc to him with each heated assault, sinking further into the bedding and bringing Marc with him. His legs wrapped around Marc's body, hugging him fiercely.

He never wanted to let go.

Marc's mouth lingering at his throat, then sweeping across his collar bone and down the centre of his chest, sent Adam's heart racing. He closed his eyes, sinking and succumbing to the moment as Marc hitched his legs up and used his tongue to drive him to a whole new level of desire. He gripped the sheets ready for what was to come;

knowing in his heart that he'd been craving this type of connection with another man all his adult life.

He gasped, crying out and arched his hips, drawing Marc in.

Oh god. Yes.

His heart thundered with an unprecedented depth of emotion as Marc rocked into him. This was where he was supposed to be.

Here with Marc.

The cool night air caressed Adam's skin as he lit up his second cigarette. It was a bit chilly with only Marc's robe to keep him warm, but he'd needed to clear his head. He wasn't sure what he'd been expecting. But having Marc possess him so completely, occupying such an intimate space, had messed with his head.

He leaned into Marc's warmth as Marc stepped up beside him.

"You alright?" Marc asked as he fought to keep the heavy blanket he was wearing from falling off his shoulders.

"Mm.... Yeah, just thinking." Adam leaned against the railing of the small balcony situated just off the loft area and took a long draw on his cigarette. "When you were inside me…" He exhaled, watching the smoke drift serenely on the wind. "I felt a little overwhelmed." A soft laugh escaped as he picked a thread of tobacco from his tongue. "And not because you were hurting me or anything. Because you *so* weren't."

"Mm…." Marc leaned in and kissed Adam's cheek. "I kind of figured that. You were making the most incredible sounds."

A shy smile caressed Adam's face. "I've never felt that close to anyone before." Shrugging, he brushed his temple against the bulky, blanketed ridge of Marc's shoulder. "But then I've never been in love like this before."

"That makes two of us." Marc grinned and nudged Adam with his shoulder. "You want to go back in there and switch things up?"

Adam flicked the cigarette away; not bothering to finish it. "Yeah?" He pulled the robe tighter around his body. "You do that?"

"What's that supposed to mean?" Marc bumped Adam with his hip, playfully directing him back towards the door. "I bottom plenty." He pressed the door closed behind them, readjusting the blanket so he could throw it back onto the foot of the bed.

"Do you really?" Adam raised an eyebrow as he let the robe slip to the floor and scurried back under the covers. He squirmed against the soft sheets that had felt so delicious against his skin when Marc had been driving him into them earlier. They were still warm from Marc's body and smelled of sex. He inhaled deeply. Intoxicating, virile, male sex. His gut clenched, remembering.

I love him so much.

Marc wedged in behind Adam, pulling him into his arms, and kissed the back of his neck, breathing softly across the little hairs.

Adam hummed, tucking in tighter to Marc's body.

I could spend forever in your arms.

"That sounds perfect," Marc said.

Adam snorted happily as colour tinged the tips of his ears. "I never had this much trouble with my mouth before I met you."

"Perhaps we can put your mouth to better use."

"Why Mister Tucker—" Adam swatted at Marc's arm and then settled into stroking it. "And here I thought you were such a perfect gentlemen." He extended his hand, clasping Marc's in his own.

Marc grunted softly into Adam's ear and suckled the edges into his mouth; his hot breath teasing a groaning response from Adam.

"Fuck… baby," Adam gasped, making Marc chuckle.

"Mm…." Marc nuzzled his face into the soft curve between Adam's shoulder blades and kissed each one of the bones along Adam's spine, starting at his hairline.

Adam sighed and rolled forward as Marc pushed him away to continue the trail of kisses all the way down to his tailbone. He was trembling by the time Marc's hot breath graced the skin of his ass and pooled between his thighs.

He shivered.

"You cold?" Marc asked. "I can turn the heat up."

"No, I'll be fine." Adam motioned for Marc to come back up the bed. "Mm… that's better," he said and snuggled into Marc's arms, tucking into the curve of his neck, and pulled the comforter back over them both.

Marc leaned away to study Adam's face. "You're not having any regrets, are you? About what we did."

Adam kissed Marc's chest and adjusted his body to fit closer against Marc's. "Not a single one. I'm just really tired."

"Okay." Marc brushed a thumb along Adam's cheek and then cupped his face and kissed him. Drifting back, he wet his lips. "I love you." A quiet smile drifted across Adam's face as he closed his eyes. It had been a very long and extremely emotional day, but he couldn't imagine being any happier than he was right then.

The smell of coffee brewing alerted Adam's senses to the fact it was morning, but the air in the room felt icy cold on his bare skin so he decided to ignore his caffeine addiction. The nicotine addiction, unfortunately, would be harder to ignore, but Marc had asked him not to smoke in the apartment, and he wasn't desperate enough to brave the cool outdoor air quite yet.

He pulled the thick down comforter over his shoulders and tucked in tighter against Marc's back, wrapping an arm around Marc's waist, and drawing a leg up onto Marc's thigh. The chill immediately left his bones. Marc's body was like a furnace; a warm and sexy furnace with a heart stopping, seductive scent. He ventured a kiss right in the centre of Marc's back.

"Hey." Marc's hand found Adam's, caressing it, then held it in place on his stomach. "I didn't wake you up, did I?"

"Why? Do you snore?" Adam teased, exhaling hotly across Marc's neck; the rumble of pleasure rolling through

Marc's body in response encouraging Adam's confidence. Somewhere in the back of his mind Adam had imagined there would be a certain amount of awkwardness between them after they'd been so intimate the night before. No one had ever explored and caressed his body the way Marc had; touching and tasting everything; loving every part of him. It had been the most erotic experience of his life.

"I've never had any complaints," Marc said, smirking.

"Um… hm." Adam sighed, breathing in the warmed air now surrounding them as his mouth found tender pieces of skin along Marc's neck to lay down soft kisses and take playful bites. Marc's hand came back and grasped onto Adam's hip, encouraging him.

"Mm… I could get used to waking up like this," Marc said.

"I usually wake myself up with a coffee and a cigarette," Adam replied, grinding up against the crease in Marc's ass. "But I think I could be persuaded to change my ways." He pressed his hand further down Marc's body, grasping Marc's cock, and began stroking it as he thrust his own shaft against Marc's body; sending his foreskin rolling back and forth over the ridge of his cockhead.

Oh fuck, that's it. Adam groaned and set his teeth into Marc's shoulder, breathing heavily down Marc's arm.

"Adam." Marc removed his hand from Adam's hip, placing it between their bodies as he directed the head of Adam's cock deeper into his crease. He rode his ass back until he could feel the pressure caressing his hole. He looked over his shoulder at Adam. "Grab the condoms from my bedside table."

Adam kissed Marc's shoulder and rolled towards the edge of the bed, lifting what he needed out of the drawer, but something caught his eye. He pulled the drawer open wider.

Oh, my goodness. Mister Tucker. You naughty boy, you.

Grinning, Adam closed the drawer and joined Marc back on the other side of the bed. He was pleased to see that Marc had rolled over onto his back. He really didn't like the idea of fucking Marc from behind. He'd only ever done that with women he wasn't particularly interested in and had no intention of ever seeing again. The last thing he'd wanted to do was see their faces while he was fucking them.

God, you were such an ass.

"What did I do?" Marc asked, wrinkling his brow.

"No—" Adam shook his head. "I was talking about myself."

"Why?" Marc shuffled up onto his elbows. "What did you do?"

Adam crashed down beside Marc and threw an arm over his face, covering his eyes. He could feel the heat rising in his face, colouring his cheeks; he felt sick. Why more of those women hadn't smacked him stupid, he would never understand. A shiver ran up his spine. He didn't want Marc finding out about his past and the way he'd treated women. It wasn't who he was; not really.

Or maybe it was. He'd certainly been consistent.

Fuck.

The condom at this point seemed pointless. He was too distracted; hovering somewhere between vomiting and passing out. He hauled the condom off and pitched it at the floor.

"Adam?" Marc struggled onto his knees. "What is it?"

"Nothing." Skirting over, Adam slipped out of bed and headed for the washroom. He pressed the door closed and leaned against the sink, looking at himself in the mirror as he ran a hand through his hair. *You're disgusting is what you are.* He turned on the water, drowning out the sound of the phone ringing. A light tapping on the door returned his attention and he finished with his toothbrush.

"Adam?"

"Yeah, just a second." Adam turned the water off and stared at his reflection in the mirror. *Never again or I'll beat you senseless myself.* He felt a little better as he headed over to the toilet to relieve himself. He would never do anything to hurt Marc.

"You alright?" Marc asked through the door.

"Yeah." Adam popped the door open and leaned against the frame. "I'm sorry for freaking out like that. There are still some things I need to work through."

"Religious stuff?"

"No," Adam said, smiling. "I think I've pretty much burned my bridge to heaven at this point."

"Adam—"

"I'm joking," Adam said, reaching for Marc to draw him closer. "I don't believe that for a second." He nestled their hips together, joining his hands behind Marc's back. "I'm past all that. But there's some other stuff I need to finish chastising myself for." He planted a solid kiss on Marc's lips. "Who was on the phone?"

"Kelsey actually."

"What did she want?"

"Your mom called her place looking for you."

Adam wrinkled his nose. "Yeah, I guess I better call my mom and let her know where I've moved to."

"Did you want the phone?"

"Thanks." Adam dropped onto the bed, but not before finding his underwear. There was no way he was talking to his mom in the nude. Not that she'd know, obviously, but it felt creepy; especially after what he'd been doing with Marc.

He took the phone from Marc, dialed, and stretched out on the bed to wait. His mom was always slow to answer, presuming his dad would get it.

She finally picked up.

"Hey, Mom."

"Adam." She sounded pleased to hear from him. "I phoned the number you gave me and that friend of yours, Kelsey, said you'd moved." The tone of her voice changed. "Why didn't you tell me?"

"I just moved last night, Mom." Adam sighed and scrubbed a hand across his eyes. Thirty four years old and his mom could still make him feel like a little kid getting scolded.

"Did you get your own apartment?"

"No, Mom. I'm sharing a place with a friend."

"A girlfriend?"

"No, not a girlfriend."

The audible sound of relief at the other end of the line made Adam grin. "It's a guy I met at the studio," he said, shifting over as Marc lay down beside him. He reached for Marc's thigh, holding onto it for emotional support. He almost hummed with contentment as Marc edged closer and tucked into him, stroking his cheek.

"Oh, I see." She paused. "Is he a ballet type friend?"

"No, Mom. He's a football player. Uncle Tom has probably heard of him." Adam squirmed in tighter to Marc, rolling into him and tracing Marc's features with his gaze. "His name's Marc Tucker. He plays for the Vancouver team. I've never actually seen him play, but I've heard he's really good."

Marc winked at him, making him blush.

"He and some of the other guys on his team have to take lessons," Adam continued. "To improve their flexibility—"

Marc's eyebrows jumped up and down bawdily.

It was all Adam could do to keep a straight face. He smacked at Marc's chest and then contented himself with stroking his knuckles back and forth along Marc's collarbone. It took him a few seconds to realize there was silence at the other end of the line.

"Mom?"

"Adam, the reason I called is because Cathy has been talking about heading out your way for a visit."

Adam sat up, shrugging away from Marc. "Is she planning on bringing Connor?" He gripped onto Marc's hand as it slid into his. To have his son visit him, and maybe even meet Marc, would be the most incredible thing he could hope for. Unfortunately, that would also entail Marc meeting his ex-wife, Cathy.

"No, she was planning on going alone," his mom replied.

Marc rested his head against Adam's shoulder when Adam shook his head *no* to what he'd asked his mom.

"Then why does she—" Adam started, questioning.

"She has it in her head that the two of you should mend things for Connor's sake. I'm in agreement with her in principle. A child should have a mother and a father; otherwise he might grow up strange like those people you see on television."

Adam bit his lip, trying not to laugh. It was anyone's guess which *strange* people his mom was talking about, but he had a pretty good idea who she was referring to given all the media attention the gay rights activists were getting at the moment.

"Somehow, Mom, I think it would be far more damaging for Connor to grow up with a mother and father who don't love each other, don't get along with each other, and have completely different views on life.

"That is exactly what I told her."

"You agree with me?"

"Cathy is a good girl, but you, you've lost your way and are drifting further and further away from Jesus. I pray for you everyday; asking the Lord to guide you back into his arms."

Adam sighed and rolled his eyes. "Thanks, Mom."

"I don't understand why you do it."

"Do what?"

"Persist in walking a path of destruction with the drinking, and the smoking… and the whoring—"

"The what?" Adam coughed, laughing and reached for the pack of cigarettes on the bedside table, snapping them up. "Did you just call me a whore?" Marc covered his mouth to keep any sound from escaping and rolled over into his pillow. Adam pinched Marc's leg affectionately as waves of Marc's muffled laughter shook the bed. He'd get him back for that later. He was pretty sure his mom could hear Marc in the background. She was sighing quite emphatically.

"Adam, be serious. Your lifestyle...." She paused in thought. "I don't think you should have *any* contact with Connor."

"Hold on! What?" Adam leaned forward, slipping a cigarette between his fingers. He wasn't going to light it, but the feel of it poised there was tempering his outrage somewhat. "Connor is my son, Mom. And I will see him as often as I want. Once I get organized, I'm coming out to visit him whether you like it or not."

"Adam, please don't be cross with me. I only want what's best for Connor. Cathy's parents are providing him with a loving home and a good Christian upbringing. He doesn't need his growing dedication to the Lord sullied by the likes of someone like you."

A gasp escaped from Adam's gut almost taking his breath away. "Someone like me? What the fuck does that mean?"

Adam's mom sighed in exasperation.

Fuck, fuck, fuck! I did not mean to swear out loud.

"So is Cathy coming out here or not?" Adam asked finally.

"No."

"Then why did you tell me she was thinking about it?"

"Because you need to understand the full consequences of living in sin the way you do. Your father and I raised you better than this. And this pain you're feeling, missing out on Connor's life, is nothing compared to the pain you'll endure in the fires of hell."

Adam fell back into the pillows. "Well at least I won't be cold." He rolled in closer to Marc and brushed a hand up Marc's chest, absentmindedly playing with the soft, dark hairs.

"This isn't a joke, son. The Bible is very clear on what awaits those who defy God and give in to their temptations."

"Mom, could we come back to saving me some other time. I haven't even had my morning coffee and cigarette yet." A sharp exhalation of air through the phone had Adam moving it away from his ear.

Oh god. Now I'm in trouble.

"Idle hands, Adam. It's nearly ten thirty where you are."

"Marc kept me up late," Adam said flicking at one of Marc's nipples and grinning, "moving my stuff in." He rubbed a thumb over the other nipple and watched it harden.

Marc grunted quietly, expanding his chest. His hand slipped down to his cock and he brushed his palm along it, pressing its increasing length into the flesh of his stomach.

Adam almost dropped the phone.

"Mom, I have to go."

"Wait, Adam. What's going on?"

"What do you mean?" Adam pitched the cigarette and cigarette package at the bedside table, missing it entirely. He wasn't going to need a cigarette anytime soon. Everything he needed was right in front of him. "Everything is fine."

"You sound different."

"I am different." Adam's gaze wandered up and down Marc's body. "I've never been happier." He caught Marc's eye and gave him a shy smile. "Mom, I really have to go."

"Alright. It was nice to hear your voice."

"You too, Mom. I'll email you the address. Love you."

"I love you too. I'll pray for you."

"You do that." Adam wrapped a leg over one of Marc's as he pressed the *end* button on the phone and tossed it to one side. "According to my mom, I'm a whore, a bad influence, and I have idle hands." He stroked the softness of Marc's belly, running the back of his hand under Marc's hardening cock, encouraging it.

"I quite enjoy your idle hands."

"Do you now?" Adam cupped Marc's balls, tugging lightly as he teased Marc's taint with his finger. Marc groaned and shifted down the bed. His legs dropped open as Adam's tongue circled a nipple; flicking and sucking it in.

"You alright after what your mom said?" Marc asked between shaky inhalations.

Adam sat up. "She doesn't think I should see Connor."

"That's ridiculous." Marc stroked Adam's arm. "I'll tell you what.… I have a lot of airmiles I'm never going to use. Once you've wrapped up this ballet performance, why don't you use them to go and see Connor?"

"Really?" Adam kissed the curve of Marc's neck, licking him delicately as he backed away. He sat straight up with determination. "Only if you come with me."

Marc blinked. "You want me to come?"

"Yeah."

"As your boyfriend?"

Adam dropped his gaze. "No. I think it would be better if you just came as my friend. My family wouldn't understand, and my parents would disown me." He slouched to one side. "And Cathy—God. She'd make sure I never saw Connor again."

"That bad, hey?"

"You have no idea."

"Then why do you want me to come?"

"I want you to meet my son."

Marc rubbed a thumb across Adam's hand. "I'd like that."

"Would you really?" Adam sighed. "You want to meet him?"

"Yeah, really. I love kids; especially if he's yours."

Adam angled in, kissing Marc with such sincerity that Marc felt like he was going to pass out.

"I love you so much," Adam said. "I honestly don't know what I would do without you."

Marc shivered. "Show me."

Adam rid himself of his *modesty for mom* underwear and reached for the lube that was still lying beside his pillow where he'd tossed it earlier. He dispensed a small amount and arranged himself to prepare Marc the same way Marc had done for him the night before; minus the tongue. He wasn't quite ready for that yet. He massaged the clenching ring until Marc relaxed a little then pressed a finger inside, remembering what it had felt like to have Marc caressing him in such an intimate way.

His own cock pulsed and hardened as the soft, smooth walls of Marc's ass closed in around his finger. The pressure was tight and warm, and felt amazing. Not the least bit strange, surprisingly; this was Marc's body and he loved every inch of it.

He drew his finger back out a ways and then slid it back in and kissed Marc's stomach. Each time he did it, the muscles relaxed and began to stay open.

Marc groaned and shifted his hips.

"Fuck that feels good," he said, reaching for Adam's shoulder.

Adam reset his position, maneuvering his body to be in between Marc's legs. "Where's that little gland thing?"

"Put another finger in first." Marc pulled his knees up, hooking them with his hands. "Keep running your fingers up towards my stomach until you—" He gasped and clenched onto Adam's arm. "That's it there." Adam kissed the underside of Marc's cock and ran the bridge of his nose along its length. It was fully erect now.

"What do I do now?" Adam asked.

"Stroke it lightly. Front to back." Marc's body arched up as he dropped his head back. "Fuck that's it." He ground his ass into the bedding as Adam alternated between stroking his prostate and fucking him with his fingers. Marc reached for his cock, but Adam brushed his hand away, taking its length into his mouth instead.

Marc's dick slipped easily in and out of his mouth. He'd refined his technique; purely in his mind, after giving Marc the blowjob in Kelsey's apartment last week. No teeth this time. More tongue; and wetter. It had to be wetter. He spat down its length and jacked Marc's cock a few times while he tongued the slit and then sucked heavily on the head.

Tastes so good.

He adjusted his position again, opening his throat and allowed Marc's entire shaft to invade the tight space. He swallowed around its girth and gagged, choking; which seemed to turn Marc on even more; his ass clenched down hard around Adam's fingers. So he kept doing it, suddenly wanting to devour Marc.

The saliva ran from his mouth in streams when he pulled back to suck at the head again. He was a mess and so were the sheets; wet with spit and lube. He sat back on his haunches to re-evaluate, slicking his fingers up again and pressing them higher into Marc's gut. He rubbed his other hand across his own chin. It was dripping with spit, his nose was running profusely and tears were spilling from the corners of eyes. And he'd never been so aroused.

He dove back onto Marc's cock.

"Adam. Stop." Marc tapped Adam's shoulder. "I'm gonna cum if you keep that up." His brow furrowed. "Unless that's all you wanted to do. You don't have to fuck me."

Adam withdrew his fingers and sucked hard on the head of Marc's cock and then flicked the slit with his tongue. He let it fall from his mouth. "Oh, no," he said. "I want to." He grinned as he used the corner of the top sheet to wipe his nose, and then climbed further up Marc's body. "I want to do everything and *anything* with you." He winked at Marc.

Marc blushed. "You saw my stash of toys, didn't you?"

"Um... hm." Adam nodded and then closed in on Marc's mouth, delving into it with his tongue, exploring the warm, wet response. He reached for the discarded box of condoms and without releasing Marc's mouth, slipped one on. He retreated enough to hitch Marc's legs up onto his shoulders and then surged forward, devouring Marc's lips. He sucked on the bottom one and set his teeth into it, drawing a small amount of blood.

Marc groaned and squirmed beneath him as Adam bit a line across his chin and scraped his teeth along Marc's jaw line to his ear; the sound and feel of Marc's morning stubble against his lips and teeth churning up his hunger. Marc's scent, taste and texture were pure male; driving his senses insane with desire.

He licked at the soft lobe of Marc's ear and pulled it into his mouth as he struggled to press his cock into Marc's hole. It finally surrendered and he slid in faster than he'd intended.

Marc grunted out a loud *fuck* and pressed against Adam's stomach, shifting his ass away from him.

"Jeez, Marc. I'm sorry." Adam brushed Marc's temple with his thumb, cradling his face in one hand. "Are you alright?"

"I'll live." Marc laughed and lifted his head to kiss Adam. "We'll just have to keep practicing until you can make a nice, smooth entry." He wrapped his legs around Adam's body and pulled him in, moaning and responding with the rocking of his own hips as Adam began a slow undulating thrust, dragging back and forth across his prostate. Marc grunted, swearing each time Adam closed in against him; the tension building faster than he would've liked.

Then Adam increased the pace, hammering into him like nothing he'd ever felt before. It was too much. Marc's stroking hand slowed, and Adam covered Marc's mouth with his own, capturing the sound as Marc's body bucked and came beneath him.

Chapter Seven

"I'm telling you," Marc said, laughing into the phone. "Adam moved in with me last night, we stayed up really late, and this morning I was too sick to go to practice." He nodded his head, grinning as he pitched through the contents of his bedside drawer. Adam had been rooting around amongst his toys in the drawer when he'd returned from the bathroom, and he was trying to determine what if anything Adam had taken from it.

"I'll tell him," he continued. "Yes, of course I'll be playing tonight. You know I'd never miss a game." Marc dropped down onto the edge of the bed and winked at Adam as he came back in the room. "Coach… I'll make sure he doesn't hurt me." He waved his hand around at Adam, chuckling over the response from his coach on the other end of the line. "Alright. I'll see you later this afternoon for warm up. I promise."

"That was a curious conversation," Adam said as he glanced over at the open drawer of the bedside table. He'd only been looking for a pen, but it was cute to see Marc thought otherwise.

"Ah, he's just bustin' my balls for missing practice."

Adam slouched against the door frame, re-tying the knot on his sweatpants. They were getting too loose for him again. He'd have to either gain some weight or buy a new pair of pants.

Buy a new pair.

He straightened up. "What time is your game tonight?"

"Four." Mark slid the drawer closed and cut his eyes across Adam's demeanor. "Did you find anything of interest in there?"

"Oh… I found *everything* of interest, but I've made us something to eat, so you'll have to question me about it later."

"Mm… sounds like fun."

"My mother warned me about men like you," Adam teased as he arranged the sandwiches he'd made onto two plates alongside an assortment of cheeses and pickled vegetables. He'd never been one for anything pickled but Marc seemed fond of that sort of thing, having quite an array of choices in his fridge.

"No, she didn't," Marc retorted.

Adam slipped into a seat across from Marc at the dining room table and sought out Marc's feet to nestle his socked ones against. Even bare, Marc's feet were warm and cozy against the chill of the apartment. They'd have to discuss the thermostat.

"No, she didn't. But she should have." Adam smiled and bit into his sandwich, chewing happily. The sandwich tasted better than he would've expected. He caught Marc's eye.

Probably the company.

"What time do you have to be there for warm-up?" Adam asked.

"I'll slide in around three."

Adam cocked an eyebrow. "That sounds a bit on the lean side."

"I plan to be plenty warmed up before I even get there."

"Mm… hm." Adam pursed his lips. Marc really was absolutely adorable the way he kept peppering him with innuendos like a string of bad pick-up lines; his eyes lighting up with anticipation each time he dropped one.

"So, are you coming to the game?" Marc asked, getting back to the business of eating. Adam was glad he'd thought to put the large dish of potato salad he'd found in the fridge out on the table as well. Marc was making short work of it plus everything else on his plate. He would have to remember to put more food out next time. A six foot four, two forty pound frame appeared to require a significant amount of sustenance.

Adam pushed the half sandwich he hadn't touched onto Marc's plate and sat back. The last time he'd made an attempt to see one of Marc's games, it had been disastrous. That was the day he'd first told Marc he loved him. And Marc had taken off running.

His belly twitched with anxiety.

"I love you," Adam said, rising from his seat and reaching for Marc. It was crazy, but he needed the reassurance.

"I love you too, baby."

There. See. No running.

Adam slipped into Marc's lap, breathing him in. Marc wasn't going anywhere. And either was he. Then Marc's lips crushed against his, and Marc's hands found their way up under his shirt, stroking his back and pulling him closer. Innuendos weren't required to know what Marc had in mind, and Adam was only too eager to follow him back to the bedroom.

He shrieked in surprise, giggling at his outburst, when Marc lifted him into his arms and strode up the stairs, past the bed and into the bathroom, depositing him on the edge of the counter as he reached into the enclosure to turn the shower on.

"Oh, my god… you scared me," Adam said laughing. "I can honestly say I've never had anyone carry me before."

Marc chuckled against Adam's lips as he pressed a light kiss there. "We need to get cleaned up," he said, stripping out of his clothing, and nodded at Adam to do the same.

Adam slipped off the counter and slid his sweatpants off his hips after throwing the t-shirt he'd borrowed from Marc's closet onto the floor. "I didn't realize I was dirty," he toyed.

Marc growled and scooped Adam up, dragging him into the shower. The cold tiles meeting his back shocked Adam's system a little, but the sensation was soon forgotten when Marc's mouth closed over his and Marc's rough hand encased both their cocks, stroking them in unison; strong and steady.

Mm… another first.

The next forty minutes was a glorious blur of unprecedented experiences and Adam's legs felt like jelly by the time Marc lowered him off his hips and back down onto the floor of the shower stall. He'd never felt so entirely connected to anyone before. Marc was quite literally *rocking his world.*

He swept Marc to the other end of the shower stall and sunk to his knees. Things were about to get much dirtier before they even contemplated getting cleaned up for the game.

The stadium looked just as it had the day Adam had been there last; right down to security guard who'd broken the start of his meltdown by telling him to get up off the floor and move on.

Adam avoided eye contact with him as he wandered reluctantly towards the box seating where the spouses, children and girlfriends of the players were supposed to sit. He'd tried to convince Marc to secure him a seat in the general admission area, not wanting to be put in a position of having to introduce himself to a bunch of strangers, but Marc had balked at the idea, stating he was one of the most outwardly confident people he knew.

Adam sighed.

Outwardly confident. Exactly.

His stomach lurched as he pressed past the throng of people hovering near the door, and made his way up the short flight of steps into the small lounge preceding the viewing area overlooking the field. He just wanted to find a seat in the furthest corner to watch the game and hope no one took notice of him. He was not prepared for the sheer volume of female chatter and laughter in the room, and the immediate onslaught of questioning eyes.

He peered up from beneath his evasive posture at the perfectly manicured features of women who could've easily stepped off a fashion runway in their high heels, short skirts and flashy jewelry. It struck Adam, as he soaked in the entire environment, that he was so far out of his element that he might actually pass out from the stress, although, he thought, the stinging scent of perfume alone was probably enough to do the trick for him. This was nothing like his world of sweaty bodies, rosin dust and quiet discipline.

"Hi, I'm Pamela." A thin, busty woman extended her hand to Adam. "And you are?"

Adam sighed, straightening up.

Come on. You can do this.

"Adam." He accepted Pamela's hand, shaking it lightly and gathered himself up. "Marc's boyfriend."

Another woman crowded in. "I hadn't heard Marc had a new boyfriend." She extended her hand. "Hi, I'm Kim."

"Hi, Kim." Adam tried to smile, but his knees were beginning to feel as if they might buckle out from under him.

"You look like you could use a drink," Pamela said, hauling Adam towards the bar. "What's your poison?"

"Um… gin and tonic, thanks."

"Watching your weight, are you?" Pamela grinned as she prepared Adam's drink. She was about to cap the bottle when she thought better of it and winked at him. "I'm making you a double. You look like you're about to pass out."

"Thanks," Adam said as he leaned into the wall behind the bar and accepted the glass. The cool ice and the alcohol slipped easily past his lips, curling warmth into his trembling gut. The soothing effect was familiar and extremely welcome.

"So, how long have you known Marc?" Pamela asked.

"Just a few weeks. I met him at the ballet studio I work at."

Pamela cupped a hand over her mouth, shrieking with laughter. "Oh, my god… you're that Adam?" She peered over her shoulder, seeking out her friend. "Kim," she shouted. "This is that *Master O'Neill* the boys were telling us about."

Adam dropped his chin to his chest.

Perfect.

"I hear you're quite the brutal task master," Pamela continued after turning back to face him.

"And pretty handy with a cane," Kim added, giggling. "I didn't know Marc was into that kinky stuff."

Oh my god… get me out of here.

"We're teasing you, Adam," Pamela said, pushing Adam's shoulder affectionately. "Are you always this serious?" She patted Adam's face. "You need another drink."

God, yes.

After downing his second double gin and tonic, Adam slid into a seat between the two women in the viewing area, feeling much more comfortable than he probably should due to the alcohol. He had to consciously fight the urge to flirt with them even though he wasn't the least bit attracted to either one of them. It was a bad habit that always reared up when he drank too much.

And I've definitely had too much to drink.

He slumped further into his seat as the game started until Pamela pointed out which player Marc was, and that perked him up a bit. He leaned closer to the railing and followed the muscular lines of Marc's powerful body as he moved about the field, remembering what that powerful body had been doing to him in the shower earlier; thrusting and grunting its way to fulfillment as he'd clung desperately to him, riding the intense, rolling wave of the most incredible orgasm he'd ever had.

He swallowed and tucked his knees together.

Fuck.

Marc had insisted he go without underwear today. He hadn't argued the point, and now his cock was pressing fervently against the rough zipper of his jeans, pinching his tender skin. The discomfort in his ass after being plundered by Marc repeatedly over the past few hours was bad enough, but this added irritation was doing strange things to his body.

It was seriously turning him on.

Marc knew this would happen.

Adam grinned as he leaned back in his seat, folding his hands in his lap to hide his obvious arousal. He and Marc were going to get along just fine in the bedroom department. His gentleman lover definitely had a twisted, adventurous streak.

He cleared the thought from his mind.

Right now, he needed to concentrate on what was happening on the field. If everything went well between Marc and him, there were going to be a lot more of these games in his future. He should at least try to figure out how the game was played.

Chapter Eight

"Did you pick up the green peppers yesterday?" Marc asked Adam as he scanned the interior of the fridge.

"Yeah," Adam turned from the stove where he was frying up some onions in a small amount of olive oil. The plan was to make curry, which they probably should've started over an hour ago, but they'd become distracted while showering and getting ready for their first official dinner party as a couple. "They should be in the crisper drawer." He stretched to see where Marc was looking. "That one there. At the back."

Kelsey slid onto a stool situated under a small breakfast bar facing the kitchen. "How are you guys doing in here?"

"If we eat by midnight, we'll be lucky," Bill, from Marc's football team, said while nudging up against Kelsey's shoulder. "Can I get you another drink?" He moved away, headed for the fridge. "Strongbow, right?"

"Yeah, thanks." Kelsey folded her arms on the counter and tried to get Adam's attention. He eventually responded to the sharp hissing sounds coming from her.

"What?" Adam asked.

Kelsey leaned closer, whispering, "Why did you invite Bill? Is this some kind of blind date or something? You know I'm not interested in guys."

"Relax," Adam said, patting her head. "Bill knows that. Marc and I just thought the two of you would get on really well as friends. That's all."

"That's all?"

Adam leaned over the counter and kissed Kelsey's forehead. "That's all. Bill is a complete nutcase when you get him wound up. You're perfect for each other." He ducked as Kelsey made a swing at his head. "Missed—" He leapt away before she had another chance to try and smack him.

"Thanks a lot, asshole," Kelsey said, shrugging further into her seat. "I should've brought Linda with me."

"I thought you two broke up?" Marc said.

Bill set Kelsey's glass down in front of her. "Yeah, I heard you two had a huge blowup."

Marc leaned across the counter and shoved Bill's shoulder.

"I asked you not to say anything," he said.

Bill shrugged. "You started it." He twisted the cap off his beer and slid in next to Kelsey. "So you're back together with Linda?"

"No," Kelsey replied. "It just slipped out. Linda and I were together for a long time. Two years. It's going to be strange not having her at my side. I'll have to finish my own sentences."

Adam flicked his eyes in Marc's direction. They hadn't gotten to that point in their relationship yet. They'd only been living together for a few months. But he could see how easy it would be to slip into something that comfortable with Marc.

He smiled shyly as Marc snuck in beside him and kissed his cheek. "Hey, you," Adam whispered.

"Are you getting excited about seeing Connor tomorrow," Marc asked as he began feeding the fry pan the rest of the ingredients.

"I'd be more excited if you were coming with me."

"I'm sorry I had to back out."

"How's your mom doing, Marc?" Kelsey asked, remembering that Marc preferred to refer to his second mom as *mom*, not Carol.

"She's holding up alright," Marc replied. "She was really close to her dad. Losing him so suddenly has really thrown her."

"I can't imagine losing my dad," Kelsey said as she cracked off a piece of the papadum Adam had pulled from the deep fryer. "Not that I talk to him very often."

"Why not?" Bill asked. "Doesn't he live in town here?"

"He does. But me and his girlfriend don't exactly get along." Kelsey took a sip of her cider. "We used to date." She shook her head when Bill's eyebrows shot up "It's fucked up. Don't even ask."

"Kelsey used to have a practice with her dad," Adam added.

"That's right," Bill said. "Marc said you were a shrink."

"Operative word being *were*," Kelsey replied. "Started to feel like a bit of a hypocrite knowing I was more screwed up then my patients. It's for the best." She slipped off her stool and headed into the kitchen. "What can I do to help? I'm starving."

"Go and set the table," Adam replied. "Marc and I will have this ready in about thirty minutes, promise." He leaned into Marc's side at the stove, bumping him playfully with his hip. Living with Marc and doing all the everyday stuff with him felt as natural as breathing, forcing him to re-evaluate his happiness scale. This here, now, was the happiest he'd ever been.

Adam gripped the back of the sofa as he descended slowly onto Marc's waiting cock, adjusting his position to take Marc in at the exact angle he was most fond of; the one that rubbed him in all the right places and made his toes curl. No amount of assurances and accolades from the other gay men in his dance troupe could've prepared him for the reality of just how *fucking* good it felt to be riding another guy's cock.

Especially a guy you were in love with.

Their guests had only been gone less than ten minutes before they'd given up on clearing away the dishes and attacked each other in the living room. Adam's flight back east to visit his son was scheduled to leave at eight the next morning, but Marc had to be up at five to catch his flight down to the States to be with his mom. They wouldn't be seeing each other again for over a week. Time to be together was of the essence and neither one of them felt like wasting it by sleeping.

Marc slid his hands under Adam's ass to help support his weight as he began his rise and fall. The sound of the phone ringing through from the lobby intercom evaded his senses for a second; being barely audible above the incredibly arousing and volumous utterances erupting from Adam's moist, seductive mouth.

"Just leave it," Adam said, gasping for breath. He dropped one hand onto Marc's shoulder and used the other to stroke himself. "I'm so fucking close… just—"

Adam sank down hard into Marc's lap, and rocked his hips, grinding Marc's shaft against his gland.

"That's it, baby," Marc said as he pulled and twisted at Adam's nipples, wetting his fingers first. "Cum for me. Let's see it."

"Fuck—" Adam convulsed forward, grabbing onto Marc's bottom lip with his teeth. He pulled it away gently, pressing his forehead against Marc's as he shot his warm load onto Marc's chest in jolting waves of release.

He relinquished Marc's lip and grabbed his face, kissing him.

"Mm…." Marc smacked at Adam's ass. "Up—"

Adam removed himself from Marc's lap, climbing off the sofa, and bent over; supporting himself by placing his hands and one knee on the massive, glass coffee table Marc had repeatedly assured him could take their combined weight. So far, so good. The table had actually become one of his favorite play surfaces. He loved the way it felt cold against your skin to start, but then heated up and became slippery with perspiration; its solid composition offering no reprieve from the force of their hips as they took turns hammering into each other.

He grunted and slid forward a bit as Marc slipped into him, then pushed back, steadying himself to take the full barrage of Marc's thrusts; waiting for that moment when he'd feel the warmth of Marc's completion filling his ass. After some discussion and an agonizing wait for test results, they'd stopped using condoms about a week ago, and it had opened up a whole new level of intimacy for them; one Adam had never felt with anyone before. Trust and commitment had become a sensual component in their lovemaking.

Adam arched his back and angled his hips, squeezing tight around Marc's cock as he felt it pulse. He reached back for Marc's thigh, pulling him in tight as Marc clutched at his waist and released rope, after warm, delicious rope, deep into his ass. Adam leaned back into Marc's body, sighing with exhilaration; not wanting to release him yet, as he tried to catch his breath.

The phone started ringing again.

Marc looked around the room. "Maybe Kelsey forgot something. She always forgets something."

"Probably." Adam pulled away, cringing as Marc slipped from inside him. A wet, sleepy reminder of riding bareback trickled its way down Adam's inner thigh as he crossed the room for the phone. And while passing the far side of the coffee table his toe caught the edge of the small, stainless, jewel topped butt plug Marc had bought him for his birthday a couple of weeks ago and convinced him to endure for the entire of the dinner party; hence the lack of patience with the tidy up; sending it scurrying under the coffee table, sparkling in the light.

"What the fuck did you forget?" Adam said into the handset.

"Excuse me?"

"Mom!" Adam covered the handset in shock, but soon found his calm, reserved voice as he scanned the room, trying to locate the bottle of lube he'd knocked onto the floor earlier. "Mom… it's almost one o'clock in the morning. What are you doing in Vancouver?" He waved his hand around, directing Marc to get dressed and start cleaning up. He was going to try and stall his mom for as long as possible. "I wasn't expecting you."

"No, I realize that."

"Why are you here? I'm flying out to see you tomorrow."

"That's why I'm here. Oh…wait—"

Adam strained to hear what his mom was saying. She appeared to be talking to someone else. Then the phone clicked off.

Oh shit!

Adam slammed the phone down. "She's on her way up."

"What is she doing here?" Marc dropped to his knees looking for his underwear, and started tossing articles of clothing up onto the sofa. He came up eye level with the coffee table; it was covered in Adam's smeary handprints and speckled in his perspiration and drops of cum. He grabbed a sock and wiped it down as best he could as Adam made a run for the washroom.

"I don't know." Adam straightened his hair in the mirror and washed his hands after throwing back a measure of mouth wash.

"Here," Marc said as he stepped into the bathroom and handed Adam his clothes. "And these…." He opened the cabinet under the sink and threw the plug and the lube in beside the towels. He grinned at Adam and kissed the back of his neck. "And, before she steps through that door, the apartment is going to reek of Febreeze and glass cleaner, I promise."

Adam looked up and met Marc's eyes in the mirror.

"Thank you," he said.

"Only for you," Marc said while wetting a facecloth under the hot water and wiping the sticky mess from his body. "I don't like hiding, you know that. But I love you… and if that's what you want, that's what I'll do."

"Marc—"

"Not now," Marc planted a noisy kiss on Adam's lips. "Get your clothes on. She'll be here any minute."

"Wait." Adam grabbed Marc's shoulder, stopping him from leaving. He cupped Marc's face with his other hand and kissed him. "I love you so much." He buried his face in Marc's neck.

Marc tipped Adam's face up to look at him. "Hey… I know you do. I understand why you can't tell your mom. It's alright."

Adam shook his head. "It's not alright. For the first time in my life, I've fallen in love." He brushed a hand up into Marc's hair, stroking at his ear. "Being with you makes me happier than I've ever been… and I can't even tell my family about you."

"Maybe someday—"

Adam shrugged away. "They're supposed to love me. How can my parents say they love me and then be prepared to judge the source of my happiness? Shouldn't they want me to be happy?"

"You know it's more than that, Adam. If it was strictly about this one lifetime, they might not have an issue with me. It's the eternal damnation stuff that has them worried. Adam, your mom and dad *do* love you. That's why they're looking out for you long term."

Adam leaned heavy against the counter. "I hate this."

"I know. Get dressed," Marc said as he rubbed Adam's back. "I'll throw on my clothes, wipe down a few things and let her in." He smiled reassuringly into the mirror. "We can do this. Alright?"

Adam sniffed and nodded. "Yeah. I'll be out in a second."

Adam wasn't too long leaving the bathroom after Marc let his mom into the apartment. She'd only made it into the front hall and was handing Marc her coat when Adam made his appearance.

"Mom," Adam said, grinning, and swept her up in his arms, kissing her cheek. "It's so good to see you." He wrapped an arm around her shoulders, hugging her in and inhaling the familiar scent of the body powder she'd been using for as long as he could remember. "Did Marc introduce himself?"

Marc laughed. "I was just getting to that." He extended his hand. "It's nice to finally meet you, Missus O'Neill—Mark Tucker."

"Please just call me Joanne," Joanne said; her eyes narrowing on Marc's flushed face as she took his hand. She clutched onto Adam's arm as she was directed towards the living room. "It's a lovely place you have here, Marc."

"Thank you," Marc replied.

"Very modern and… high end."

"Oh, well—"

"Is Adam paying his fair share?"

"Mom—" Adam wrapped his arms around his chest; reduced to a child once again by his mother.

Why does she do this?

Marc scratched at his head. "Um… yeah. There's no mortgage, so it's just utilities and stuff. And then we split the food seventy thirty." He chuckled. "Adam doesn't tend to eat very much."

"That's because he smokes too many cigarettes."

"I don't, Mom," Adam said, biting at his thumbnail. "I've cut way back since I moved in with Marc."

And you don't want to know what I'm substituting them with.

"So, what are you doing here, Mom?" Adam asked as he motioned for his mom to take a seat. "Why didn't you just call?"

Joanne looked around at the offering of furniture and decided on a stiff, high backed chair near the window. "I needed to have a word with you in person before you flew home."

Adam slid onto the small coffee table beside his mom and reached for her hand. "Is there something wrong with Dad?"

"No," Joanne answered. "Your dad is fine."

Adam's face sunk and his eyes became open and sallow. "Is there something wrong with you?"

"Oh, heavens, no," Joanne said as she patted Adam's hand.

"Then what is it?"

Marc stroked a hand across Adam's shoulders. "I'm going to start the kettle for tea."

"Thanks, hun," Adam said absently and turned back towards his mom, whose eyes were now scanning the room with frantic disbelief. Adam swiveled to see what his mom was looking at. Marc had definitely cleared away the toys they'd been using, and he'd tucked their rather vast selection of porn videos out of sight. The loft was visible, but it wasn't obvious that it was the only bedroom.

And then Adam's gaze came to rest on the bookcase.

There were no less than eight framed photos of him and Marc taken during the day trips they were so fond of. They rarely managed a day when they were both off work, so when they did eke one out, they liked to make a special day of it by going somewhere. Some of the photos were taken during hiking trips through picturesque national parks, others ocean side and a few were taken downtown at various coffee shops and restaurants with friends. It was more than obvious that they were together.

"What is the meaning of this?' Joanne said, standing up and heading for the bookcase.

"Mom, I can explain." Adam looked towards the kitchen, searching for Marc, but he was fussing with the kettle and hadn't heard what was being said.

"I don't understand," Joanne said as she lifted a picture Kelsey had taken of him and Marc during the New Year's Eve festivities. They were standing in the middle of a crowd of people, entwined in each other's arms, locked in a passionate kiss; completely oblivious to the fireworks display happening in the sky above them. Kelsey had drawn little hearts all over the picture in red grease pencil.

"Mom—" Adam repeated, following after her and sinking down onto the back of the sofa. "Mom, I'm in love with him."

Joanne set the picture down. "No."

Adam scrubbed a hand through his hair. "Yes, Mom, I am. I'm in love with Marc and he's in love with me." He peered over his shoulder. Marc had spotted Joanne with the photo in her hand and had wandered back into the living room. Adam tried to shift away from Marc when he set a hand on his shoulder, but his position on the back of the sofa wasn't giving him enough room to do so, and he didn't want to be too obvious about it; even though Joanne was refusing to make eye contact with either one of them, choosing to pick threads loose from her sweater instead.

Her breath caught as she spoke, sucking in a soft, wet inhalation.

"It's an abomination," she said.

"Mom, it's not. I love him." Adam stood up and Marc's hand drifted down his back, hooking onto the band of his jeans. "I'd never been in love before I met Marc. All those women… they meant nothing. It was all meaningless. But the first day I set eyes on Marc...?" He shook his head remembering how Marc had turned his insides to jelly that very first morning in the ballet studio. "I knew we were meant to be together." His mom looked up and he scanned her expression; his eyes pleading with her to try and understand. "I've never been so happy. Please, Mom… can't you just be happy for me."

Joanne clasped her hands together so tight the colour of her knuckles mottled. "You gave in to carnal temptation with this man, nothing more. Adam, please. Think about what you're saying."

Adam shrugged away from Marc. He appreciated Marc's support, but the touching wasn't helping. It was obvious that it was making his mom uncomfortable.

"This isn't about sex, Mom. This is about me being in love with another human being." Adam ducked his gaze away from his mom's tear filled eyes. "I won't lie… the sex is important, but I'm in love with Marc because of *who* he is, not *what* he is."

Joanne straightened out the front of her skirt and fussed about with the buttons on her sweater. "Well," she said with a steady and eerily disinterested tone. "I ought to be going. My flight leaves early tomorrow morning and I'll need to find a hotel for the night." Joanne stared straight up into Marc's eyes. "Because I won't be staying here... in this perverse den of iniquity and sin."

"Joanne—" Marc started, but Adam placed a hand on Marc's chest to stop him from speaking.

"Don't," Adam said. "There's nothing you can say."

Joanne raised her hand as she stepped around Adam and Marc, headed for the front door. "I'll let myself out, thank you."

"Mom, wait...." Adam reached the door ahead of Joanne and placed his body in front of her. "You never told me why you flew all the way out here to talk to me in person."

Joanne donned her coat and tucked her hands into her pockets, closing herself off from any more of Adam's embraces. "Cathy has found herself a new husband," she said. "He's from the church and he's a lovely man, willing to overlook Cathy's prior relationship with you. But he isn't interested in raising another man's child, so Cathy's parents have agreed to adopt Connor."

She set her stance, slightly uneasy. The colour from Adam's cheeks had washed away, leaving him pale and listless, and Marc had swept up behind him, wrapping his arms around Adam's waist to keep him from slipping to the floor.

"They'll need your permission, of course," she added.

"Over my dead body," Marc said and kissed the top of Adam's head. "I'll be contacting my lawyer in the morning. But I guarantee you—Adam won't be signing any adoption papers."

"This has got nothing to do with you," Joanne replied.

Adam blinked, staring at his mom and then turned to face Marc.

"My mom's right," he said. "This has got nothing to do with you. Connor is *my* son. I'll decide what's best for him."

Chapter Nine

The flight was awkward in its stubborn silence between them, but now that they were in the rental car on their way to Adam's parents' house, Marc couldn't contain himself any longer.

"I thought I knew you," he started, "but obviously you've been hiding the fact that you're actually a cold, heartless bastard."

Adam slammed his hand against the steering wheel, grimacing as pain shot up his arm. "Drop it! This is none of your fucking business, Marc." He turned and glared at him. "Why did you come with me? Shouldn't you be with your own family?"

"Fuck off, Adam—" Marc threw himself around in his seat to face him. "We've been through this a million times. You *are* my family. Don't you understand that?"

"No. Actually I don't."

"Bullshit." Marc grunted and looked out the window at the passing scenery. "You're so fucking stubborn."

"Look who's talking."

"Don't start that again—"

"I'm not starting anything." Adam redirected his attention back on the traffic. He could've driven this road in his sleep having lived in the same house all his life, but he hadn't been to his parents' house since the Christmas before last and some new traffic lights had been added, throwing him off. That and he wasn't used to driving, not having owned a car in years.

Fuck, I can't concentrate.

Adam narrowly avoided a pedestrian as he pulled off the road onto the shoulder, and Marc freaked, gripping his armrest, and turning on him; his face flushed with disbelief. "Jesus Christ, Adam! What the hell are you doing? I told you to let me drive."

"Don't change the subject."

"I'm not changing—Fuck! You almost hit that woman!"

"So now you're saying I'm a bad driver and a bad father?"

Marc dropped his head against his headrest. "Oh. My. God. I have never met anyone so exasperating in my life."

Adam sucked in a shattered breath; his emotions hovering somewhere between tears of defeat and blinding fury. "Then why would you want *me* to be a part of *your* family, seeing that I'm a cold, heartless, stubborn, exasperating bastard with enough baggage and emotional hang ups to bring us both down?"

Marc threw his hands onto his face. "Because you're also the man I'm in love with. And I didn't mean half of what I said."

Adam's lip twitched. "What about the other half?"

A snort of amusement escaped Marc. "Every fucking word."

"Hm." Adam exhaled, smiling, and relaxed. "I won't ask which half." He sunk into his seat. "Can we talk like grown men now?"

"That would be welcome change after the last fourteen hours."

Adam ducked his eyes. "I'm sorry, but see, the thing is, Marc," he started, while picking nervously at his thumbnail. "I can't take care of a child. I'm not equipped for that kind of responsibility. I work ridiculously long hours. I smoke and drink far too much, and I can't even feed myself half the time, never mind a growing boy."

"So we'll enroll Connor in preschool and hire a sitter for when we're not home, and I can make sure he gets enough to eat. The other stuff... we can work on together."

"We?"

"Yes, we."

"Mark—" Adam slouched into his head rest. "Connor needs stability in his life. Do you really think we can offer him that?"

"Why couldn't we?"

Adam sighed with exasperation. "We've only been together a little over three months. He's not a puppy, Marc. We can't just drop him off at the pound if we split up."

Marc shrugged his arms into place across his chest.

"I'm not planning on going anywhere," he said and looked up into Adam's eyes. "Are you?"

"Of course not, but—"

"Why are we any different then other couples with kids?"

Adam's eyebrows shot up.

"Um—we're not married for starters," he said. "Or even common law for another nine months…. Remember, Connor isn't your son. He's mine. Which means until we're married, common law or otherwise, you could walk away and leave me with no way of supporting Connor on my own. There would be no equal division of assets, no spousal support… nothing."

"That's harsh, Adam. I wouldn't do that."

"You don't know that."

Marc scrubbed a hand across his face and stared out the window. "I want all that with you... to be married."

"Yes, so do I—eventually. But we're not ready to take a step like that. Not yet."

"So, you're just going to let Cathy's parents have him." Marc turned away from the window; his face twisted with anguish. "You're going to abandon your son and let some people you don't even know raise him? You're his father. You have a choice."

"God, Marc...." Adam reached for Marc's arm, but Marc pulled away. "This isn't the same as what happened to you. Connor has been living with Cathy and her parents since he was five months old. He knows them, probably better than he knows me."

"It doesn't matter. He's your son."

A heated rush of anger flooded Adam's face. "And Cathy's his mother, Marc! What about her?"

"What about her? She's abandoned her son and married some fucking moron from the church. A man who will undoubtedly treat her like shit because she's nothing more than property to him."

Marc swiped at his face and then reached for Adam's hands. "Please, I'm begging you. Don't do this to Connor. Don't let him grow up thinking that neither of his parents loved him enough to keep him around." He lowered his gaze. "At least I knew both my moms loved me. I knew I was wanted—that it was the system keeping me away from my home."

"Connor knows I love him. He'll always know I love him."

Marc looked up. "How Adam? Are you going to send him birthday cards with little hearts? Maybe fly out for Christmas and give him a hug? Buy him an extra present when you can't make it?"

"I talk to him on the phone every day."

"That's admirable. But it's not good enough, Adam."

Adam shut his eyes and leaned his head against Marc's shoulder.

God, he's right.

"That's not how kids measure love," Marc continued. "They measure it in bedtime stories when they can't sleep, in cold cloths and hot water bottles when they're sick, in being held and listened to when they're sad, and in you being there, laughing along with them when they're happy." Marc brushed his thumb in circles on Adam's wrist and then slipped down, gripping onto Adam's hand. "It's the day to day stuff that counts. We can do that for Connor."

"You really want to do this?" Adam peered up into Marc's face. "You want to do this with me?"

"Of course I do." Marc grasped Adam's chin and kissed him, only relinquishing a whispers distance as he released his mouth. "I don't think you fully realize just how much I love you."

"I think I do." Adam drew back, restarting the car. "We'll talk more tonight."

"Thank you." Marc slipped his hand onto Adam's thigh, squeezing it affectionately. He sat up straighter as they approached a house that was obviously full of guests; there were cars parked everywhere on the street. Adam pulled the car up the driveway and around to a small parking pad beside the garage.

"Who do you think is all here?" Marc asked.

"Well, being that it's Connor's birthday… I would guess both sets of grandparents, his great aunts and uncles, some cousins and a shitload of family friends." Adam turned and looked at Marc. "And we'd be pulling Connor away from all that if we moved him away."

Marc cast his eyes downwards.

"Marc." Adam touched Marc's chin, encouraging him to look up. "It's one of the downsides. But we'll weigh everything out tonight after the party. I just wanted to draw your attention to it."

Marc nodded his head. "I know." He sighed and looked up. "Do you think your mom is expecting us?"

"*Us*? No. And I'm sure when I didn't show up at noon she assumed I'd slept in and missed my flight. Probably breathed a sigh of relief that she didn't have to deal with me."

"It was important that you spoke with my lawyer this morning."

Adam reached for Marc's hand. "I'm glad you talked me into it."

"You didn't seem glad at the time," Marc said and laughed. "You looked like you wanted to rip my head off."

"Never." Adam clung to Marc's face and gave him a quick, noisy kiss. "You're head's too cute."

"Mm—" Marc grunted, winking at Adam. "Which one?"

Adam smacked Marc's arm and swung his door open. "Mister Tucker, has anyone ever told you, you have a one track mind?"

"Is that a problem?" Marc said as he retrieved the football he'd had all the guys from his team sign for Connor, from the back seat. He followed Adam up to the front door. "Because last time I checked, that was one of my redeeming qualities."

"Oh, and it is," Adam said as he nudged Marc with his shoulder. "And we'll explore that further back at the hotel, but right now—we're at my four year old son's birthday party. So behave."

"So, am I behaving as your *boy* friend, or your *best* friend?"

"I don't know." Adam pushed the door open into the front hall. "I doubt my mom has told anyone about us. We should probably just lay low, hang out with Connor and eat some cake."

Adam peered into the living room to see who was there. Both of his parents had siblings, unlike himself. His mom had two sisters, who were both there with their husbands and their myriad of adult offspring and their subsequent children. His dad had two brothers and a sister. It appeared that only one of the brothers, his Uncle Tom, and his wife had made the trek out for the party. He couldn't see his dad's sister, but she was likely around somewhere; she only lived a few doors away.

"I think *coming out* at my son's fourth birthday party," Adam said, "would probably rank pretty high on the *faux pas* list."

"Whatever you decide. I'll just follow your lead."

"Thanks, hun."

Adam took a deep breath and encouraged his face to brighten as an elderly couple approached. "Auntie Mildred," he said, allowing the rotund woman to pull him into her arms.

"Adam... your mother said you couldn't make it," Mildred said, stepping back and holding Adam's face in her hands. She kissed him square on the forehead. "I'm so pleased to see you. You're still as handsome as ever. But always so skinny. You need to eat more. Doesn't he, Tom?" Mildred peered over her shoulder at her husband, who was clasping his hands together excitedly at the sight of the person standing behind Adam.

"Yes, dear," Tom said as he stepped around his wife and Adam, and extended his hand to Marc. "Marc Tucker. Well, I'll be. What brings you all the way out here from the West Coast?"

"Um," Marc stammered. "I'm here with Adam. Just tagging along for the ride."

"So you really are rooming with our Adam," Tom replied. "Joanne told me you were, but I thought maybe she'd heard wrong." He jabbed at Marc playfully. "I couldn't imagine a sporting man such as yourself finding common ground with a ballet dancer; enough to share an apartment anyways."

"We get on just fine," Adam said as he shimmied up to the frame of the door leading to the kitchen, pressing his back against it as he caught Marc's eye. "He makes me leave all my dancing gear at the studio though. He says it gets in the way."

Marc grunted and redirected his eyes away from Adam's shy, cock warming gaze, and back onto Tom's expectant face.

"You're a football fan then," he said to Tom.

"Oh, yes, um—" Tom rolled his eyes. Joanne was barreling towards them from the kitchen.

"Adam?" Joanne said, gripping Adam's shoulder from behind.

"Mother." Adam crossed his arms and turned on his heel to face her, and leaned back against the door frame. She did not look pleased to see him. "I'm sorry we're late. *We* had a few things to do before *we* could leave, so *we* caught a later flight."

Joanne's gaze cut across to Marc. "I thought you'd planned on coming alone. This get together is for family only."

Adam extended his hand towards the living room in irritation. "Then why are all your friends from the church here?"

Joanne exhaled a sharp hiss. "They've known Connor since he was born. They *are* a part of his family. They've certainly spent more time with him than you have." Her eyes flicked back at Marc. "I'm going to have to ask you to leave." Her gaze snapped back onto Adam. "Both of you. You're not welcome here—"

"What on earth, Joanne?" Mildred said as she wrapped an arm around Adam's shoulder. "What has gotten into you? You can't kick Adam out of his family home on his son's birthday. He's making an effort…. He flew all the way out here to see him."

"This is no longer his home," Joanne stated without a hint of emotion. "Adam made his choice to follow Satan into the fires of hell. I will not have him dragging Connor along with him."

"Now, Joanne," Tom said, scanning the large gathering of people listening in, looking for Joanne's husband Michael. "Let's just calm down a minute."

Marc stayed put, questioning Adam with his eyes, but Adam just shook his head. He didn't want to make the situation worse by having Marc rush to his side. A tug at Adam's pant leg caught his attention and he turned and dipped, lifting Connor into his arms.

"Hey, boo." Adam planted a solid, wet kiss onto Connor's cheek.

"Daddy... you wanna come see all the new cars I gots."

Adam scrunched up his face comically, making Connor giggle. "You got more cars? That's not possible, boo. When I talked to you on the phone last night, you told me you had like... thousands."

"No—" Connor patted at Adam's face. "Silly." He pressed his palms into Adam's cheeks, making Adam's lips pucker, and settled a tiny kiss on them. "I say hunreds."

"Oh, hundreds... well, that's different." Adam winked at him. "Where are these new cars then? I want to see them." He slipped past Joanne with Connor still in his arms. She wouldn't dare say anything more while Connor was with him. He stopped and turned, jerking his head at Marc to follow along, and headed out across the living room, wading through the curious stares.

Connor wrapped his arms around Adam's neck.

"Who's the big man?" he asked Adam.

"That's Marc, honey."

"He looks nice."

Adam stopped and peeled Connor away from his neck, studying his little face, then peered over his shoulder at Marc.

He is nice.... He's more than nice.

"Did you want to meet him?" Adam asked Connor. When Connor nodded, Adam turned back around to face Marc.

"Connor," Adam said. "This is Marc... daddy's boyfriend."

Connor giggled. "You has a boyfren?"

Adam looked around at the open mouthed reactions of his family, and reached for Marc's hand, gripping it fiercely. With Marc at his side he could get through anything; even this.

"Yes," Adam continued. "Daddy has a boyfriend and he loves him very, very much." There was complete silence around him, and an uneasy feeling lodged itself in his stomach. He cringed as his dad leapt up from his chair and took off into the front hall.

God please don't let this be a mistake.

Connor eyed Marc, pinching his face up as he concentrated on Marc's features. He reached forward and poked Marc in the chest. "You like to play cars?"

Marc grinned. "I love to play cars. I used to have a yellow pickup truck with black stripes that wrapped—"

"Oo… I has one too." Connor slipped out of Adam's arms and reached for Marc's hand, hauling him into the adjoining family room. Marc peered over his shoulder and winked at Adam.

Oh my god. They're adorable.

"Looks like Connor's found a new victim," Tom said as he stepped up beside Adam and patted him on the shoulder, directing him away from the living room and into the back hallway away from prying ears. "Adam, don't let your mother push you around like that. I figured you and Marc were together when she first told me about you two moving in together. Marc doesn't exactly hide his *preference* from the sports world."

Adam smiled, relieved. "Thanks, Uncle Tom."

"Although, I didn't realize you were that way… what with all the women and everything."

"Yeah." Adam laughed softly. "I didn't either apparently."

"Marc's a decent guy though, hey? I've seen him giving interviews on television. He seems alright."

Adam grinned, shyly, darting his eyes up in Tom's direction. "He's more than alright. I've honestly never been happier."

"Good. The main thing is you're happy."

"Thank you. I can't tell you how much I appreciate having someone from the family on our side. I think we're going to need it." Adam leaned against the wall. "Marc and I have been discussing taking Connor home with us."

"Oh, Adam… I don't know about that."

"Why not?" Adam watched Tom's changing expression, seeking a hint of what was running through his uncle's mind.

"What you and Marc have going on—it's a bit of fun and all that, but you can't bring a child into it."

"A bit of fun?" Adam coughed out a laugh of disbelief. "Marc and I are in love with each other. Not thirty minutes ago we were discussing getting married someday. This isn't just a bit of fun."

Tom crossed his arms tightly across his chest. "Adam, I'm all for you gays having your rights and everything, really I am, but I don't like the idea of raising a child in an environment like that."

"An environment like what?" Adam's voice escalated. "Are you afraid Connor might see us cooking dinner and doing laundry together? Perhaps watching the news on television? Taking a walk in the park? Or worse yet, working to provide him with a loving and supportive home to grow up in! Is that what you're afraid of? Well, fuck you, because quite honestly, he'd be damn lucky to have two parents that are prepared to do everything in their power to make sure he grows up healthy, strong, and well adjusted!"

Adam clenched a fist and pounded it against the wall behind him as he fought to contain his rising temper. "Which is more than I can say for Cathy's narrow minded, bible thumping parents! Because, god forbid, that poor kid turns out to be gay like his old man! They'd probably pitch him out on the roadside just like my own mother is prepared to do to me!"

"Adam." Marc slid in beside Adam and placed his hand on Adam's back. "Baby, I can hear you clear out to the family room. And so can Connor. You're scaring him."

Shit.

Adam turned into Marc's shoulder as Marc wrapped an arm around his waist, and shuddered through an exhalation.

"Shh… it's alright," Marc said, cupping the back of Adam's head. His fingers easily found the spot that if caressed had an immediate calming effect on Adam. "Let it go."

"I don't think I can do this," Adam whispered. "I don't know anything about raising a child. I'm fucking up already."

"You're not fucking up. You're upset. You're allowed to get upset. Connor's just worried that you're sad, that's all."

Adam shut his eyes, letting the soft rise and fall of Marc's chest soothe him. "I can't do this without you."

"I told you I'm not going anywhere."

"God, I love you."

"I love you too, baby."

Adam turned back. His mom and Cathy's parents had crowded into the hallway beside his uncle. He hadn't meant to draw attention to himself like that, but now that he had….

"Um…" Adam started. "Marc and I have been talking. And we've decided that Connor is going to come live with us—"

"What?" Cathy's father pushed in front of everyone.

"It's not open for debate," Marc said. "Cathy has already relinquished her parental rights to clear the way for you to adopt Connor, leaving Adam as Connor's only legal guardian, and he's not signing anything. Connor is coming home with us."

Adam sighed with exasperation. He loved Marc without hesitation, but he was finding that Marc had a tendency to let testosterone rule his behaviour, and would often assume the role of *the man* without giving any thought to the fact his partner was perfectly capable of handling his own affairs.

Most of the time.

Over the course of the three plus months they'd been together, there'd been more than a few power struggles between them. But so far they'd managed to work things out. Adam just hoped Marc's need to take charge wouldn't spill over into their decisions on raising Connor, although he trusted Marc's judgment far more than his own when it came to kids.

Marc loves me. We'll work it out.

Adam directed his attention on Cathy's mom. "We'll pick Connor up at your place tomorrow morning. Please make sure he has enough clothes and toys to last him until you can ship the rest of his stuff out to us. And we'll need his birth certificate—"

Adam pulled away from his mom when she grabbed his arm.

"Stop it," he said, brushing her aside.

"You can't do this," Joanne said. "You're not fit to raise a child."

"Most people aren't, Mom. But Marc and I are going to do our best. I promise you that."

Joanne shook her head. "It's not right. Two men, like *you*, bringing up a young boy. I can only imagine…."

Adam opened his mouth to start into a string of obscenities, but Marc beat him to it, and Adam was left to use his raging adrenaline to stop Marc from leaping at his mother instead.

"What the fuck is wrong with you?" Marc shouted, surging forward; his immense body almost toppling Adam over. "He's a child. What kind of sick fucks do you think we are?"

"Marc, stop." Adam pressed his back into Marc's chest, holding him in place. "Fuck!" He stumbled as Marc shoved at him again. "Marc, stop! You're going to hurt me."

"Fucking bitch!"

"Stop, Marc!"

"But—she can't just…."

"Just stop. It's pointless." Adam turned and placed his hands on Marc's chest. "Pointless, Marc. Nothing you say is going to change the way she thinks. I've been dealing with this my whole life."

He caught Marc's gaze. "Alright?"

There was a flash of something in Marc's expression that made Adam's stomach drop, but the blow to the back of the head caught Adam completely by surprise. This was his home. This was supposed to be his family. It had all gone wrong. He'd fallen in love and it had all gone wrong.

The image of his father clutching the butt end of a rifle didn't come into focus until he was sinking onto the floor at Marc's feet.

His knees hit first, jarring his sight, and then he crumpled, tipping against Marc's shins.

He stared up at the man that had raised him; a man that was supposed to love him like he loved Connor.

The gun was in motion again.

Marc was screaming and tripping over his body.

Then everything went black and blissfully silent.

Chapter Ten

The throbbing pain in Adam's head surged into his temples, tightening the muscles in his neck. He clenched his eyes shut and rolled onto his side, hoping a different position would alleviate the pain radiating from whatever injury he'd sustained at the studio. He couldn't even remember what he'd done.

What time is it?

Trying to lift his head turned out to be a mistake; a shard of sheer agony streaked up through the back of his skull, peeling the serenity off his stupor, and he cried out, reaching for Marc.

"Marc?" Adam's hands clawed at the sheets beside him, but the bed within his reach was empty, and it was too dark to see. He scrambled forward looking for him; his hands grasping at the pillows and shoving them aside.

"Marc!" he shouted through gasps of tears.

"Shh... baby. I'm right behind you," Marc said as he tucked himself closer. He draped an arm over Adam's waist, embracing him, and hugged Adam tight against his hips, knowing it was the position that brought Adam the most comfort when he was having a rough night. Fitful nights of sleep had become the new norm for them since Adam's dad had attacked him two weeks ago, but tonight was particularly bad. Adam had been waking up repeatedly over the past couple of hours. His headache wasn't showing any signs of relenting and Marc had already topped out on the amount of pain medication he could give Adam for another few hours.

Marc lifted the cold pack from the pillow where it had fallen and replaced it on Adam's forehead, and pressed a soft kiss into the apex of the bristly regrowth of hair on the back of Adam's head. The stitches were out, but the headaches and nausea stemming from the severe concussion sustained in the blow were persisting, leaving Adam feeling hopeless and scared. They'd flown back to Vancouver a few days ago, and being home had definitely improved Adam's mood, but having to leave Connor behind in Cathy's parents' care for the time being, in conjunction with his father's betrayal, had sunk Adam into a deep depression.

Adam cleared his throat, attempting to push past the dryness.

"Can you get me some water?" he asked Marc.

"Sure thing." Marc rolled back and lifted the glass of water he had waiting on the bedside table. He adjusted the straw and helped Adam to sit up. Even the slightest movement sent Adam's head spinning, but the doctor had said the dizziness should go away eventually; the flight home had been an absolute nightmare.

"Fuck." Adam gripped Marc's arm, digging his fingers in. "I think I'm going to throw up again." He settled against the headboard, clutching the bowl Marc handed him.

"I can't imagine you have anything left in your stomach."

Marc brushed the tips of his fingers through Adam's sweat dampened hair and then traced down along his jaw line. Adam's cheekbones were more prominent than he'd ever seen them. He'd lost a lot of weight. Weight he could ill afford to lose.

"Did you talk to Connor?" Adam asked. He set the bowl down after dry heaving a few times, and leaned his head against Marc's shoulder, sinking into it.

"Yeah. I was given the full rundown on the toy situation at his preschool. Apparently, the doll to car ratio isn't to his liking."

Adam exhaled a tired laugh.

"He sure likes his cars," he said, slipping back down onto his pillow. "Did you call the studio again for me?"

"Yeah, I did. They've found someone to replace you as Romeo." Marc shuddered through the whimper that escaped Adam's lips. "Baby, you'll dance again."

"You don't know that. I can't even stand up without puking my guts out." Adam reached out for Marc's leg. "What if this never goes away? What if this is it for us? Spending the rest of our lives with me in bed, and you taking care of me." He squeezed hard on Marc's thigh. "I don't want to live like this, Marc."

"Don't start that again." Marc leaned in and kissed Adam's forehead. "We'll get through this. Whatever happens, we'll make it work. You need to suck it up for Connor's sake, alright?"

Adam smiled as he stared up at Marc.

"I wish I could see the new house," he said.

"You'll see it plenty when we move in." Marc stretched towards the foot of the bed, searching through a pile of papers for his cell phone. "I have some more pictures." He lay down beside Adam and held the phone up so they could both see.

"Is that the dog run you were talking about?" Adam asked, touching the screen to enlarge the picture.

"Yeah. It starts in the back corner of the yard—"

"Which side? I'm all turned around."

"When you come out the sliding glass door from the kitchen it's off to your right, and it runs all underneath that hedge of trees."

Adam nestled his head in closer to Marc's.

"Are you sure we want to get a dog?" he asked as Marc continued scrolling through the photos on his phone.

"Connor was insistent."

Adam grinned. "And you're just going to give him whatever he wants?" He laughed. "You're a pushover, Marc."

"Maybe." Marc turned and kissed Adam's cheek.

"We need to watch our money now that I'm not working."

"I know… we're all good. Just let me take care of things." Marc set the phone down. "I'm sorry. I'm doing it again."

"It's alright. I'm not exactly at my best. Just keep me in the loop." Adam snuggled in, wrapping an arm over Marc's chest, enjoying the way it rose and fell with Marc's breath; the combined movement reminding him of how closely they were connected.

"Do you need a cigarette before I tuck you back in?"

"No—" Adam dragged a hand across his face.

"How about a pee? I could grab your bottle thingy."

"No, Marc! Fuck!" Adam clenched his teeth. He hadn't meant to yell. He knew Marc was just trying to help and he loved him for it, but ever since the head injury his anger control had been a bit flakey, and his mounting frustration level wasn't helping any. Yet another thing the doctor had said should correct itself.

"I'm sorry," Adam whispered, embarrassed, and tucked his face into the curve of Marc's neck, kissing it. His skin was warm and the scent so familiar to him, it helped to relax him again.

"It's alright. You can't help it." Marc's fingers traced a line up Adam's arm. "Do you still love me?"

Adam smiled against Marc's neck. "Of course I do."

"Mm… then I have something else to show you." Marc struggled free of Adam's arms and slid open the bottom drawer of his bedside table and removed a small, white satin pillow. He straightened up and handed it to Adam.

"What's this for?" Adam asked, turning it over in his hands. It was definitely too small to use behind his head.

What the fuck is he up to now?

"Connor and I had a little discussion on the phone tonight in addition to pondering the car dilemma at his preschool."

Adam stroked his fingers across the smooth satin fabric and flipped the pillow over again. He had a sneaking suspicion where this conversation was going and it set his pulse racing, making his head swim a little as he set the pillow on his stomach.

"And what did you discuss?" Adam's face flushed. He licked his lips and focused on Marc's face now looming above him.

"We were discussing how handsome he'd be as our ring bearer." Marc shuffled closer. "I know we said it was too early to think about getting married… but I almost lost you. And now we've bought a house together. And Connor is coming to live with us in less than a month. And—"

"Yes."

Marc stopped.

"Yes, Marc," Adam said, reaching for Marc's face. "I'll marry you. As soon as I'm able to stand up and take my vows without falling over and throwing up, I'll marry you."

"What if I carried you in with a fancy ass barf bowl?"

Adam laughed. "That works too."

Marc rushed at Adam and grasped his face, kissing him with such an intense ferocity that if Adam hadn't already been lying down, it would've dropped him to his knees.

"Careful, hun," Adam said. "You're going to make me pass out."

"Mm… I just love you so much," Marc crushed his lips against Adam's again, gentler this time. Releasing Adam's face he leapt off the bed. "Connor is going to be so excited when he hears you've said *yes*. I'm going to phone him."

"Marc," Adam said, laughing. "Tell Connor tomorrow. It's the middle of the night. He's sleeping." He patted the bedding beside him. "Come back to bed. I'm tired, my headache is finally fading, and I want to fall asleep in my fiancés arms."

The most amazing smile lit up Marc's face and Adam's own features softened at the sight of him.

How the hell did I get so lucky?

"I ask myself the same thing everyday, baby," Marc replied, grinning when Adam rolled his eyes at having spoken his thoughts aloud yet again. It was pointless trying to control it.

"Are you sure?"

Marc sunk down beside him. "About what? That I'm the luckiest guy ever, having you in my life."

Adam blushed. "How can you say that? Look at me."

"Exactly." Marc leaned in and laid a kiss on Adam's nose. "When I look at you, I see the man I'm hopelessly in love with. The man I want to spend the rest of my life with."

"Mister Tucker, I do believe you have taken leave of your senses. And I couldn't be happier about it."

Chapter Eleven

The light filtered into the bedroom through the sheer curtains as the late summer sun set behind the hills. It was only just past eight o'clock but Adam had decided to retire early. He wasn't particularly tired but tomorrow was a big day.

It wasn't everyday you got to marry the man of your dreams.

The wait had just about done them both in emotionally, but the decision had been made to wait until they'd moved into their new house and Adam's health improved before walking down the aisle together. Adam's headaches still made the occasional appearance but they were becoming fewer and further between, and the nausea, thankfully, had tapered off to the point he was able to teach classes again, but not enough to perform. Doing pirouettes almost always landed him in the washroom with his face over a toilet.

The loss of that side of his career hadn't actually upset him as much as he thought it would. He enjoyed teaching, and the set class schedule left him with more time to hang out with Connor. The frantic days of waking up at four in the morning to hit the studio, and not leaving until he was too physically exhausted to continue, were over, and he honestly didn't miss them.

Adam peeled the t-shirt and boxers he'd been strolling around in from his body, leaving him free to the air; a sensation he loved, but had put aside after Connor moved in with them. Marc had set up a studio in the basement for him to practice in, but he preferred the barre Marc had assembled in the bedroom; their one and only clothing optional environment.

He smiled, remembering the experiences they'd had in the penthouse, just the two of them; especially on that darn coffee table. He sighed, laughing. They'd had a lot of fun together and the spontaneity had suffered somewhat with the new living arrangement, but neither he nor Marc would change it for the world. They loved having Connor in their lives.

"What are you thinking about?" Marc said as he stepped up behind Adam and scooped him up, scaring a small shriek from him.

"Sure. Give me a heart attack the night before our wedding." Adam turned and circled his arms around

Marc's neck. Their foreheads met and Adam brushed his nose against Marc's. "Now, Mister Tucker," he said, deliberately letting his breath sweep across Marc's lips, warming them. "I'm fairly certain we agreed to sleep in separate beds tonight."

Marc's tongue slipped along Adam's bottom lip, and dipped in, just enough to tease Adam's mouth open, leaving them both breathless and trembling. He slipped a hand down onto the small of Adam's back, and traced a finger down the naked crease of his ass. "Who says I was planning on sleeping?"

"I was hoping you'd say that." Adam moved closer, straddling Marc's thigh and pressing his hardening cock against Marc's boxers, caressing the fabric and the soft hairs fanning out from beneath it, leaving behind wet smudges of his increasing desire. A light tapping on the bedroom door broke his attention.

"Daddy Marc?" a small voice said from the far side of the door. Adam laughed and cocked an eyebrow.

"What is it, Connor?" Marc replied. "Daddy Marc is busy."

"I can't seep," Connor answered, followed by more knocking. "I need you read me 'nother story."

"I read you three already."

"But I still can't seep."

Adam dropped his head onto Marc's shoulder, trying not to laugh. "Maybe you're just excited about the wedding tomorrow," he said and then rushed his hands up into Marc's hair and kissed him. "I know I am," he whispered.

"I twy again," Connor said, sounding a little defeated.

"Thank you, Connor," Adam replied and then launched himself at Marc's mouth again.

"Daddy?"

Adam's forehead came to rest on Marc's. "Yes, boo?"

"I wuv you."

A groan escaped Adam's lips. "Run back to bed. I'll be right there to read you another story."

"And I'm the pushover?" Marc said laughing.

Adam scanned the floor for his boxer shorts as he pulled his shirt back on. "He's probably a little hyped up after the rehearsal dinner. It's a big deal for him, us getting married."

Marc sat down on the edge of the bed. "You're going to sleep in his room tonight, aren't you?"

"He needs me."

Marc raised his eyebrows at Adam and pouted.

God, he's adorable.

"I know you need me too," Adam said, leaning in and giving him a quick kiss. "But you'll have me all to yourself for a whole week when we go away on our honeymoon."

Marc growled and wrapped his arms around Adam, falling backwards onto the bed with him. "Who'd have thought it would be Cathy's parents who would be around to help us out so much."

Adam snorted out a laugh.

"I still can't believe they actually moved here."

"They love Connor."

"Mm… that's nice, isn't it? That he still has one set of grandparents in his life."

"And my mom is pretty taken with him as well."

"Yeah, she sure is."

Adam snuggled into Marc's chest, wanting to enjoy the moment of serenity for a little longer. They'd managed to build a pretty good life for Connor so far. He had two parents that loved him, and each other. Three grandparents who doted on him to excess and two crazy aunts that lived to take him on outings to the park; Kelsey and Linda had mended things between them.

He kissed Marc's chest, smiling as Marc grunted in response.

Life was good.

No. Life was great.

Adam hummed contentedly, stroking his cheek against the soft hairs on Marc's chest. This here was it.

Lying with the man he loved the night before their wedding.

In their own home.

With their son *hopefully* asleep in the room down the hall.

And the support of the people that meant the most to them.

This here.

This was the happiest he'd ever been.

Love him so much.

Marc kissed Adam's head, chuckling. "Love you too, baby."

****

About the Author

As a teen, growing up in Vancouver, BC (Canada), Leigh Jarrett spent many hours each day discovering the stories surrounding the many characters emerging from the proverbial closet in her mind. Of course the adults called it daydreaming, but that didn't deter her from weaving increasingly diverse storylines as she grew older. Notes were made and pictures were drawn, but none of the stories were ever written down until she received a nudge from an unlikely source. Her imaginary childhood friend, Sebastian of Cardin, became the first written character, appearing in all three books of the Circle Trilogy. Sebastian's passion for life and the beautiful men he shared it with inspired Leigh to tell his story.

And that is where it all began.

To learn more about Leigh Jarrett, please visit:

Blog: www.leighjarrett.com

Or send an email to: author.leighjarrett@gmail.com

You can also find Leigh Jarrett on Facebook and Twitter

2621820R00108

Printed in Great Britain
by Amazon.co.uk, Ltd.,
Marston Gate.